Confessions of a
Nerdoholic

Savannah Blevins

Confessions of a Nerdoholic

Limitless Publishing, LLC
Kailua, HI 96734
www.limitlesspublishing.com

Formatting: Limitless Publishing

ISBN-13: 978-1-680258-961-0
ISBN-10: 1-68058-961-X

Dedication

To all the girls who traded
a Friday night out for a book.

Chapter One

ADMISSION

The library.

I sucked in a deep breath, taking in the beloved scent of aged, crisp paper, combined with dust and freshly brewed coffee. There was something about the library—the atmosphere—that spoke to me. It reached down to the deepest depth of my quirky girl soul and sang like a nightingale. The library understood me better than anyone else. It recognized my need to be a part of the whole, while satisfying my desire to be alone. I'd always loved the library, even as a young girl. The books, filled to the brim with stories and adventures I could enjoy in the safety and restricted confines of my room. At home I had to follow a long list of strict rules, but here, among the stacked shelves and free Wi-Fi…I could rule the world.

Eyeing my usual spot in the back left corner, across from the long row of computers, I took a quick detour to the coffee cafe. It wasn't Starbucks,

1

but it served varying shades of brown stuff for budget minded caffeine addicts. I eagerly bounced on my heels as I waited in line, mentally calculating my choices, even though I'd revert back to my usual mocha standby. I enjoyed pretending to be an actual coffee connoisseur in the same way I pretended to be a normal college freshman.

Normal had never been my forte.

I picked at the floral printed tights underneath my bright purple skirt. I hated tights. It didn't matter the brand; they caused me to itch like a dog with fleas. But I liked to wear pants even less and with the nippy spring weather in Maryland, I had to resort to the dreaded things so I wouldn't freeze to death. The weather was the one thing I missed about Hollywood. I scratched the back of my leg with the heel of my shoe with the same enthusiasm a bear might scratch his back on a tree. The judgy girl in front of me turned around to stare.

I tucked my chopped off waves behind my ear and stared back. "Can I help you?"

She eyed me a moment, resembling the pissed off turtle on her shirt that represented our college mascot before turning around with a roll of her eyes.

I got that a lot. I probably still had flour on my clothes or icing on my face. Then add on my unusual wardrobe, Marilyn Monroe hair, general dislike of people, and I was bound to catch a few odd looks. It was normal…for me.

It wasn't my fault I spent my morning perfecting recipes for the bake shop I planned to open when I finally managed to graduate with my business degree instead of attending frat parties, singalongs or whatever regular college students did. One of the many things my father expected me to do at college was pay my own rent since I begged him to let me leave the dorms, and working early mornings and late evenings at the Sugar Cube bakery was my meal ticket. It was also my passion.

I reached into my purse and pulled out my clunky black compact which depicted the wedding scene from *The Little Mermaid* on the cover and used the mirror to reapply my cherry red lipstick while I waited. The barista called out my name.

"Queen Amidala!"

"That's me." I held up my hand, the sparkly bangle bracelets falling up to my elbow. I stuck my compact back in my purse and stepped around the guy in front of me. The girl next to me stared again. And again I stared back at her. "What? You don't give them fun, fake names?"

She pretended not to hear me this time.

Weirdo.

The barista handed over my extra giant coffee. I cradled the steaming cup of ecstasy in my hands and made my way to my seat, already smiling as I sat. Today was Monday. Mondays meant I worked at Sugar Cube until noon then met my friends for a brief study session before laboring my way over to the other side of campus for night classes.

It sounded like any other day in the life of a broke college student, except today was *Monday*!

I mentally threw confetti in the air. I would have danced and started a *High School Musical* scene, but I didn't want to spill my coffee. The point was…Mondays were the best.

Besides all the normal stuff, today held one special, week-defining difference.

My deep, dark secret, that until this year, I'd managed to keep secluded in the farthest corner of my fantasy vault. It wasn't until I met my friends Sloan and Ava at orientation back in the fall that they prodded the confession out of me. I leaned back in my chair and took a deep breath as I prepared myself for the admission.

I liked a very specific type of guy.

I, Eloise Duncan, had a thing for nerdy boys.

Skinny jeans and comic book t-shirts. Black rimmed glasses and hair that never followed the rules. Forget a flashy car. Show me those A's on your report card.

Hundreds of students passed noisily by me on their way to class or to a private, quiet corner in which to torture themselves. I, on the other hand, sat in the back corner of the main study hall amidst all the action. I threw my books across the desk in front me, papers crumbled in small piles here and there, while my thirty-pack of new pencils rolled where they may. It was my way of pretending to study.

I had no intention of actually studying.

Studying was the last thing I had on my mind at the moment. A logical person might be tempted to ask why would I walk seven blocks from my apartment to the library—in death heels, mind you—to sit at a desk and not study? Lucky for me, I had a very reasonable, at least in my mind, answer. It was all due to the *numero uno* nerd of my dreams sitting about twenty feet in front of me.

I didn't know his name, but he also had his books thrown out in front of him. Unlike me, though, he read them. Line by line. Word by word. Advanced chemistry and physics were his torture of choice today.

Yes. I had been nerd stalking him for weeks.

It all started when I sat at the computer checking my email one day. Deep in my free Wi-Fi daze, I caught the sight of his chemistry book as he passed by me. Well, technically, it was his glorious backside that caught my attention, but the chemistry book definitely upped the appeal. Unfortunately, that was all it took. One glance at a pair of faded skinny jeans, and I was hooked. Shoot me up, max out my credit cards, pawn off my own dog hooked. I needed some form of intervention. I could already see myself on Dr. Phil explaining how it all started.

"Well, Doc, first it was the pants. They were really tight. Then he walked right by me. It's only polite to scope out the scenery when they flaunt it right in your face."

"But, Eloise," Dr. Phil would say, "it's not just the pants, is it?"

I'd shake my head remorsefully and maybe even let out a regrettable sigh. "No, Doc, it's not just the pants. It's the glasses too."

"Tell me, Eloise," he would insist seriously, "tell me what the glasses make you want to do."

That would be when I would break out into full Tom Cruise mode, jump on the couch, and start singing like a crazed maniac about love, puppies, and magic unicorns that leave boxes of nerdy boys on your doorstep at night.

I rubbed my temple and shook my head at my overactive imagination. I cupped my hand over my eyes and stared at him from underneath my jittery fingers. His tousled brown hair stuck out in every direction today. I wanted to run my hands through it and…pull. Then, on top of that, every two minutes he would take his finger and push his little, adorable glasses back up his nose. I growled and clenched my free hand on the edge of my seat. Weeks of desire and admiration bubbled inside of me.

I had a real problem.

"Down, tiger. You look like you're ready to pounce."

I didn't need to turn around because I already knew the teasing voice belonged to Sloan, my snarky angel of a best friend. The long sheath of her shiny black hair dangled effortlessly over her shoulder. Sloan was this tiny, pixie-like Latin goddess. Instead of acknowledging her, I kept my eyes on the unbearably beautiful boy and the way he bit his lip as he concentrated on his book. "He's wearing a tie today." I halfway moaned each word as she sat down next to me. "A freaking tie, Sloan."

A mocking smirk spread across her face. "It's just a tie, Elle."

I groaned again. Sloan didn't understand the fine qualities that made up a lust-worthy, intelligent, "make you want scream the periodic table backward" kind of man. No, Sloan had her own preference.

Cowboys.

Good, old fashioned, howdy y'all, cowboys. She found her solace lusting after Preston McCoy, the southern gentleman of her wildest fantasies who worked down at the local coffee shop next to our apartment complex. We stalked him on Thursdays.

"You don't get it." I rolled my eyes even though we'd already had this conversation twice this week.

"You're completely right. I don't get it." She turned her head to the side, scrutinizing my nerdalicious goodness. "I don't get the allure of the glasses. I mean, he's definitely hot, don't get me wrong. Throw some boots and a ten-gallon hat on that boy and I'd be saying ride 'em cowgirl, if you know what I mean."

"Yes, Sloan. I always know what you mean." I laughed and returned my attention to the object of my desire as he so perfectly turned the page in his book.

Another chair pulled up behind us. "Oooh, a tie. No wonder I heard Eloise's ovaries growling from outside."

"Don't tease her, Ava." Sloan giggled and gave me a just-joking elbow into my side. "You're very close to being correct."

I grunted my displeasure at them. Ava Morrison, goddess of all things born with a y chromosome, at least in her own mind, was my other best friend. She also did not understand. Ava was your typical all-American beauty. She walked around ready to accept her homecoming queen crown seven days a week. Ava liked her men big and beefy with a letterman jacket. Ava got her fix from Brad "if I had any more muscles I'd turn green" Helton. Brad was the captain and resident hunk on the Maryland baseball team. We had plans to stalk him every home game.

"Come on, Elle." Ava shook my arm, her eyes round and pleading. "At least find out what his name is."

"I'm perfectly fine not knowing," I said, almost freaking out at the mere idea of walking up to him.

I didn't do that kind of thing—talk to people I didn't know. Normally, I didn't talk to people in general, but strangers were a definite no. Make that stranger the cute library boy and, well…words refused to form in my mouth. I would never be able to control myself in such close proximity anyway. I'd end up grabbing him in some fan-crazed bear hug, or poking him somewhere inappropriate and embarrass myself. Because that was what I did when I interacted with regular civilians—I embarrassed myself.

Sloan propped her chin in the palm of her hand, thinking the situation over. "You could go ask him if he has an extra pocket protector or something."

"Or," Ava said, bouncing in her seat at her apparent brilliant idea, "ask if he knows what the weather is like outside."

Sloan and I looked at her. "There is a window right there," I said, pointing out at the bright sunshine beaming in through the glass.

Sloan smiled and patted Ava on the back. "Oh, Avie-bug. You better be glad you're pretty."

Ava huffed, but I already had my attention back on my nerd. He tugged at the knot of the tie, and I whimpered. Sloan and Ava sniggered loudly.

I glared at them. "You two ruin this for me, you know that?"

It was time to go to our actual study group anyway. I chucked what was left of my coffee in the nearest waste bin, and then started slamming my props shut so I could stuff them in my bag. The third slam was followed by two very high pitched gasps. I glanced up, not at the girls, but at the boy across the room. A pair of big blue eyes stared at me through thick lenses.

My nerd.

He saw me.

Me.

My limbs forgot the meaning of movement and little heart-eyed tweety birds sang Whitney Houston ballads around my head. I stared back at him because I couldn't look away. One long second later his gaze dropped back down to his book. It was only then I finally managed to make my mouth and voice work. "Sorry."

It was barely a feeble squeak, easily buried beneath the low thrum of chatter around us.

"Go now." Sloan frantically shoved me forward two feet. "You got his attention."

I only huffed and finished cramming my books into my backpack. Heat filled my cheeks. That all too familiar wrench in my gut at another social failure. "No, what I did was embarrass myself. Again."

It wasn't the first time I'd done something stupid in front of him. I spilled hot coffee down my cleavage last week, and yelped like it had taken my head off. Then my books fell off the table, and I almost flipped my chair over backward as I tried to scramble away from the burn. He'd looked at me

9

then too. Unimpressed by my wackadoodle antics.

I picked up my stuff in horrified silence. I grabbed my backpack and started to run off with the Bobbsey Twins tagging along behind me. Sloan caught up with me first. "You didn't embarrass yourself. He totally gave you bedroom eyes."

"Bedroom eyes?" I scoffed, jumping up the flight of stairs, three steps at time. "More like 'why don't you shut up so I can study' eyes."

"Give it up, Sloan." Ava sashayed up the steps beside us. "Elle's got her hots in a knot. You know there is no dealing with her when she's like this."

Sloan growled. "All right, fine. We'll change the subject. What are you doing tomorrow evening? I have my eye on some new knee high black boots. I think it's what I need to catch Cowboy Joe's attention this Thursday." Sloan struggled to catch up to me. She grabbed my arm, pulling me to a halt. "I know you only have class until ten."

"I have work after class." I stomped up a few more steps. "I have to get some extra cash if Ava wants us all to buy season tickets to freaking baseball."

"Yes." Ava squealed with excitement. "Go earn that money, because we've got some hunky monkey to scope out next week on that trapezoid thing they play on."

"It's a diamond, Ava." Sometimes I really worried about her. "It's not that hard, honey. We learned shapes in preschool."

Sloan stepped in front of me to cut off my escape. "If you must go to work, then go. But I will see you Thursday at the coffee shop, though, right?"

"Yes." I sighed because I knew there would be no getting out of it. Unlike me, Sloan was determined to land her fantasy boy one way or another. "Just don't hump the boy's leg off before I get there to hold you back."

"I'll try." She shot me her innocent smile, but it wasn't convincing. Wicked wasn't something you could cover up. "It depends on how many times Cowboy calls me Miss Sloan in that little chicken fried accent."

I rolled my eyes, stepped around her, and hopped up the last step. I tried not to think about my screw-up and focused on getting to our study group. I needed to get my English paper finished before I had to leave for work. I made a promise to myself I would only allow thirty minutes of nerd appreciation each day, and I'd reached my limit about ten minutes ago. I sighed at the thought of that tortuous tie, but reminded myself there would always be tomorrow.

Chapter Two

SUGAR CUBE

There are good days, like when your favorite nerd decides to bring a lollipop to his study session and you get the glorious pleasure of watching him lick it for forty minutes. Or when your boss buys you a fancy blender and your new blackberry icing recipe turns out extra creamy. Those were the really good days. Those were the days that made you want to get out of bed in the morning. Then there were the bad days. The really bad days…like today.

I stared at my alarm clock, my eyes blinking methodically as my mind attempted to convince myself that I was dreaming. Because it had to be a dream. A horrible Nightmare on Elm Street sequel. The longer I stared at the blank clock on my nightstand, the tighter the knot in my stomach became. Of all the mornings for my alarm to finally decide to roll over and go to things-that-annoy-me hell, it had to be this morning. Of all the classes I could have been late for, it had to be anatomy.

I pulled my pillow over my face and screamed into it as if Freddy Krueger really was after me. My grade sucked in my anatomy class. It wasn't because I couldn't cut it—I had quite the impressive academic record—it was just hard to study anatomy out of a textbook when you knew the real, much more glorious thing sat in the third seat from the right, at the fifth table, on the first floor of the library.

It was my piss poor luck that I went to the library for "nerd appreciation hours" right after my anatomy class on Mondays. So, every Monday, I sucked it up in class because I was so excited about seeing him that I couldn't concentrate, which meant my grade was currently sucking it up as well. Now I would be late for the one day out of the week that I actually paid attention.

I unraveled myself from my Hello Kitty blanket cocoon and stomped into the bathroom. No matter what I did, or how fast I rushed through my morning routine, I wouldn't make it on time. I still hurried, though, as if my father stood behind me in his usual drill sergeant fashion, lecturing me about punctuality. I brushed my teeth and grabbed the first thing in my closet. I pulled my hair around in a funky side braid and tucked it under the hood of my rain jacket, because, of course, it was raining.

Didn't it always rain on the bad days?

Normally, I walked the seven blocks to campus, but today I would have to fight the good fight with campus parking. I didn't pay the fifty bucks for a student tag, which meant I'd probably get a ticket. It would be my third one this semester, but I could get

13

four tickets before they booted my car, so it would be a worthy sacrifice.

The science building was the farthest away from the parking lot. No amount of raincoat or cursing could save me from my squishy shoe fate. I managed to get thoroughly drenched. I looked like a cat someone shoved in the gutter. I walked in with twenty minutes remaining in the class. I should have skipped, but I was a glutton for punishment. I could still hear my father's voice in my head, giving his lecture about the "kind" of people who skipped class and how I wasn't that "kind" of person, even though he somehow managed to make it sound that way.

As soon as I crossed the threshold, Mr. "I haven't gotten laid since the 1960s" gave me his usual "you don't meet my intellectual standards" glare. Except today he followed it with a very snarky, "Well good morning, Miss Duncan. It's nice to see that your fifty-eight midterm average has inspired you to become a more dedicated student."

I probably could have let it pass. I probably *should* have let it pass. However, he stood there with his gangly old man beard and brown argyle sweater looking way too smug at the embarrassment he thought he had caused me. Unfortunately for Mr. Decrepo, I was born with the smartass gene attached directly to my ego. I trotted over to my usual back row seat, set my soaking wet backpack on the desk with a splat and smiled at him. "Well, it's nice to see your erectile dysfunction hasn't affected the stick up your ass."

I realized it wasn't the best decision I'd ever

made, but that was only after he kicked me out of class...permanently.

I spent the next three hours of my already horrible morning at the student services office changing my schedule.

Should it have taken three hours to change one class?

No.

But the people working there were so lovely, they felt the need to make me sit and wait an hour before I was worthy of their attention. Finally, after surviving their judginess at my situation, they transferred me into another section. The desk lady, with pictures of a thousand cats, practically slung my new schedule at me. Scanning the sheet, I slumped around the counter. I'd been transferred into the section everyone else refused to sign up for because the lab was at six o'clock on Friday afternoon.

For the non-bar hopping lovers out there, which included myself, a six o'clock Friday night class really didn't pose that big of a deal. However, Ava so kindly explained to me that, apparently, Friday nights were Ladies' Night down at Rowdy Randy's Pub. Hence the entire reason Ava refused to let me sign up for the afternoon section in the first place. She would be crushed I would no longer be able to take part in her favorite sporting event—Friday Night Who Can Be First To Get A Hunk Drunk.

Ava was currently the reigning champ or the pub slut, depending on how you wanted to look at it. I really didn't see the challenge in it. Maybe I wasn't the competitive type, but it seemed to me that if you met the high standards of having a vagina you were pretty much guaranteed to score some points or some crabs.

Yep, I would really miss Friday nights at Rowdy Randy's.

I tried to be positive. I honestly tried to convince myself that maybe my bad day would only last until lunch. I strolled into work with a positive attitude. The thought of baking had that effect on me. Forget oysters and chocolate. Cream cheese icing was the number one aphrodisiac. The giant kitchen at Sugar Cube was my sanctuary. The scent of frosting released every ounce of tension in my body.

I couldn't wait to have my own bakery. My own little escape from the outside world. I would hire someone to be the face of the shop, meet with potential clients, and work the cash register. I would stay in the back, away from the beady eyes of society, and bake. And bake. And bake.

I would specialize in cupcakes. Gretchen, the owner of Sugar Cube, told me I had a gift. It took one bite of my famous strawberry cheesecake icing and she hired me on the spot.

I trudged through the back door of the bakery like a drowned rat. Gretchen stood at the counter, hands and torso covered in flour, applying an intricate pattern to an off-center wedding cake. Her gaze shot up at the horrendous sight of me. "Uh oh. What happened?"

Gretchen was everything I wanted to be. She was the successful owner of a magnificent bake shop. She had perfectly plain brown hair that was totally tamable on a daily basis, and most importantly, she was a social butterfly. She was a lovely type A personality with the added bonus of a top notch kindness gene.

I let my backpack drop to the ground. "Don't ask."

Her smile was soft as she motioned toward me with her spatula before sticking it in the bowl next to the cake. "No, let's hear it. I can't bear to let you walk off with that look on your face. You look like a teddy bear that lost all its stuffing."

I started wringing water out of my braid. "I woke up late, and showed up late for class."

Gretchen set a bag of icing down on the counter. "And then?"

She knew me too well. "And then the professor smarted off to me, and I said something extremely inappropriate. Well deserved, but inappropriate."

Gretchen wiped her hand across her forehead, smearing flour across her face. "Let me guess…it was Dr. Howard."

"You would be correct."

Gretchen shook her head. "That old fossil needs to retire. He used to torture me, and that was fifteen years ago."

I blew a wet string of hair out of my eyes. "Well, now I get to go to lab on Friday night."

Gretchen walked over and slung her arm around me. Water dripped to the floor out of my clothes like I was some life size human sprinkler. "Take a few minutes and get cleaned up. Then meet me out front. I want to show you something I'm working on."

Gretchen had that mad scientist look on her face.

17

It was the same look she had when she hired me. I nodded solemnly and dragged myself to the bathroom. I stood under the hand dryer in an attempt to dry the end of my dress that my jacket didn't cover. The silky black skirt with yellow trim was one of my favorites. It reminded me of the one Olive Oyl wore in all those Popeye cartoons. The material would dry easily with time, but my black ballet flats—they would be annoyingly squishy all day. When I finally made my way back out to the bakery front, Gretchen stood next to one of the long glass cases.

The other day, the case held a variety of candy, but today it sat completely empty. That was when I saw the sign that sat on top. It was new. White, trimmed in cotton candy pink. On it, in spiraling black letters, was the phrase, **"Cupcakes by Eloise."**

My mouth dropped open. "Is that for me?"

Gretchen's smile widened. "You've earned it."

I ran over and stared down into the empty case. "What does this mean?"

"It means I want you to start growing a name for yourself. Your cupcakes bring in customers to my shop on a daily basis. You should get rewarded for that." Gretchen stood back and showcased the sign like a model on the Price is Right. "You will not only get your salary rate, but you will receive a small profit from every cupcake you sell here. A small, but necessary thank you for helping my business grow these last six months."

My fingers clutched at my heart. "Wow, Gretchen. I don't know what to say."

And I didn't. This was an amazing opportunity. A chance to get my name out in the world. It felt like a start to an all too familiar daydream.

"That smile on your face is enough," Gretchen said with a laugh. "I'm glad I got to make your bad day a little better."

"This made everything about today worth it." I cupped my hands around my face, thinking of the possibilities. "I don't know where to even begin."

"How about that recipe for double chocolate everything I saw you working on last week? I definitely want to try some of those."

A smile instantly popped on my face. "You've got it."

I hurried around the side of the counter, but then doubled back. I grabbed Gretchen in the biggest, squishiest bear hug of all time…and I hated hugging people. "Thank you. Thank you. Thank you. This is by far the nicest thing anyone has ever done. I won't let you down."

Gretchen patted my cheek. "You deserve it, Eloise. Don't ever forget that."

She gave me a gentle shove back in the direction of the kitchen. "Now, go have fun."

I spent the next two hours baking and perfecting my chocolate cupcake recipe. I even used chocolate sprinkles on top and added a dollop of fudge in the center. Forget Midol, those things were like PMS hand grenades. They'd cure anything. I placed them in the case, and I couldn't stop smiling. My cupcakes had always been in the cases, but now it had my name on it.

I'd never been so proud of myself. All those

awards on my mantel back home—those had been for my dad. This, though—baking and everything about it—was for me. And I loved it.

I glanced up at the Willie Wonka-ish clock on the wall. I had time to make one more batch of something else before my shift ended. I quickly made my way back into the kitchen and snatched up my recipe book. It was just a small, flower covered journal I'd picked out of the sale bin at the thrift store, but now it held all my cupcake secrets. I flipped eagerly through the worn pages as the bell above the entrance dinged. Gretchen greeted the customer, so I stayed focused on my task.

I ran my finger down the page for my blueberry delight icing when the conversation out front caught my attention. "Yes," Gretchen said, "this is the same girl who makes the strawberry cheesecake ones you like."

"That looks like a lot of chocolate."

It was a male voice. I perked up, not because it was a boy talking about my cupcakes, but because someone in general seemed as excited about the thought of my chocolate cupcakes as I was. The admiration and excitement was evident in the chipper tone of his voice. I slipped my recipe book underneath my arm and eased over to the door that led out to the main room. Gretchen stood behind my cupcake section of the display case, but I still couldn't see the customer on the other side. "I'll take two," he said, and then he stood.

My knees locked in place and the recipe book fell to the floor.

It was the boy from the library.

The boy.

The tie and cable knit sweater he had on yesterday was gone. He sported a long sleeve red and black flannel shirt that set off his dark glasses. His hair glistened with raindrops. The water in my shoes turned to steam as my heart beat rapidly in my chest.

Library boy ate my cupcakes?

He actually wanted two of them.

Gretchen leaned across the case to grin at him. "Getting one for your girlfriend too?"

His gaze dropped to the floor and he smiled sheepishly. "No. Both are for me, I'm afraid. I'm a pretty horrible cook. If it wasn't for your bake shop and the Japanese eatery next to my apartment, I'd probably starve."

Gretchen laughed, and I sank a little lower to the floor and silently squealed. He didn't have a girlfriend. I kind of figured that because I'd never seen him talk to anyone at the library, but the confirmation felt nice. Really, awesomely nice.

I did the Macarena in a circle.

"I'll box these up for you," Gretchen told him and disappeared around the corner.

I made sure I remained unseen from my spot behind the doorframe. He walked around the shop, looking through the glass cases at the variety of delights Gretchen made. He looked at the cakes, the ten different types of fudge, and even the homemade lollipops, but he always came back to my cupcake case.

Mine.

It had to be a dream. Some torturous nightmare

21

that would end any second, leaving me alone and depressed amid my Care Bear sheets.

Gretchen returned with a bright pink box and opened the case to retrieve two of my cupcakes. I watched as she took his money and handed over my treats. He tucked them safely under his arm, gave her a friendly wave, and disappeared out into the rain.

When the door swung shut, I finally started to breathe again. It was real.

So *very* real.

I tiptoed out until I could see Gretchen and motioned for her to come to me. I wasn't capable of walking that far yet. She grinned instantly. "See," she said, pointing toward the empty door. "I told you your cupcakes are a hit!"

"Yeah," I said, barely managing to get words out of my mouth. I pointed a very shaky finger at the door. "Do you know him?"

She followed my finger. "No, but he comes in at least once a week to buy your cupcakes."

Something insane fluttered inside of me. A loved-crazed ninja with heart nunchucks that tried to fight its way out of me. "Once a week?"

How in the world had I missed that? Shouldn't my nerd radar have gone off? A twist in my panties. *Nerd Alert. Library boy in the vicinity. Repeat. In the vicinity.*

"Yep. You're becoming quite popular with the college crowd." Gretchen looked so terribly proud of this accomplishment.

I let out a small, almost hysterical laugh. Me, popular? "So, you don't know his name?"

"No." Gretchen's eyes narrowed slightly. She studied me closely, the concerned line of her lips turning up at the edges. "Do you want me to figure out his name? Or perhaps...introduce you?"

I grabbed the counter. "No. No. No."

Gretchen laughed. "Eloise...are you blushing?"

No. I wasn't blushing. I was dying. The mixture of embarrassment and pure joy combined into a toxic poison that slowly started to suffocate me. Gretchen put her arm around me. "If you like the boy, why don't you come out and talk to him next time?"

Oh god.

The dryness.

All the dryness in my throat.

"Why?" I looked incredulously at her. "Why don't you go jump off the top of the Empire State Building? Because it's scary and you'll probably die from it."

Gretchen squeezed me tighter. "You're a beautiful girl, Eloise. And you're smart, funny, and I'm pretty sure you could cook and bake any boy into a food coma. He wouldn't stand a chance."

I smiled back at her. "Thanks. I appreciate that." Then I remembered how the girl in the line at the coffee café looked at me yesterday. I was odd Eloise. Always on the receiving end of peculiar stares and awkward glances. I wasn't the kind of person you could simply throw in someone's face. I was too bold for that. I had to be introduced slowly. Carefully. Maybe not even at all. Then, of course, there was my father to consider. Even though I tried not to allow the thought of what he would do if he found out I was "wasting time" on a boy enter my thoughts. "I think I'd rather stick to providing him with cupcakes for right now."

Gretchen nodded. "Well, you let me know if that changes."

I gave her a quick salute before retreating to my happy place. I picked up my recipe book, but I could no longer focus on my next project. All I could think about was my still nameless nerd sitting at his spot in the library enjoying my double chocolate everything cupcakes.

I threw another cup of flour in my giant mixing bowl. Screw Mondays. This was the best day ever.

Chapter Three

COWBOY

I rode the euphoria of my cupcake nerd fantasy for the next two days. It made it nearly impossible to study in between classes and work. To make matters worse, my father called. Bartholomew Duncan was in his usual mood. Cranky with a hint of do-what-I-say. He wanted to know why he hadn't received a copy of my midterm grades yet. Of course, he told this to my voicemail because I didn't answer my phone.

We hadn't had a real conversation for weeks. Not since the lecture about my major. It wasn't a fight, because you didn't have fights with Bartholomew Duncan. He told you what to do, and you did it. End of story. I'd spent my entire childhood under the thumb of his tyrannical rule, and I grew weary of it a long time ago.

He didn't know that I specifically requested my grades to be sent to my apartment address, and nowhere else. He couldn't see that fifty-eight anatomy grade. I would have to tell him…eventually. However, I hoped I could ace a couple quizzes first, then recalculate my grade before I admitted to him that his high standard of a perfect 4.0 college career for me was a dream.

It wouldn't matter, though. He made it very clear when I defied his wishes and moved across the country that if I didn't keep my grades up, he wouldn't pay my tuition at Maryland next year. He'd make me come home and follow in his footsteps at Pepperdine. He would continue to try to control my major, my career choices and my dating life.

He thought my dream of owning a bake shop was laughable. Literally laughable. "Wasted potential" was the exact phrase he used to describe it. I absolutely had to bring my grade up. I wouldn't survive back in California with him. I wanted to graduate from Maryland like my mother.

The thought of her made me choke up. My father always accused me of being too much like her. Apparently, that was my biggest problem. Odd Eloise was a genetic trait. According to my straight-laced, "wear a suit even on the weekends" father, my mom was eccentric. That was the word he used, which didn't sound bad except for the way he said it. Like it was some kind of curse word or deadly disease that didn't have a cure. I could never blame my mom for leaving him.

Hadn't I left him at the first available opportunity?

The part that hurt wasn't that she left my father, but that she didn't take me with her. She left me behind. I could have traveled the world with her. I could have helped her live out her artisan dream that my father suppressed for their entire marriage. We could have escaped him together.

She was the one who taught me to bake. I couldn't help but think, every time I put a spoon in a bowl, how different my life might have been if I could have followed her. She could have spent her mornings painting, and I could have baked. We could have been the dynamic mother-daughter duo in a tiny loft apartment in some European city.

Except we were not. I hadn't seen her in over ten years. No phone call. Not even a letter.

By the time I was supposed to meet Sloan and Ava at the coffee café on Thursday, I was in desperate need of a mental and emotional break. I had a nightmare the previous night that I woke up in a dorm room at Pepperdine with my dad as my roommate. He'd switched my major to pre-law and bought me an entire closet full of pantsuits.

I walked down the street toward the coffee shop with my heels clicking together like Dorothy from the Wizard of Oz. They were the same color and just as sparkly. If I clicked them enough, I might transport myself back to the bake shop and relive Library Boy buying my cupcakes all over again. I skipped into the coffee shop, forcing my mood to lift so my friends wouldn't ask questions, and allowed the warmth to surround me. I slipped off my jacket, straightening out the fluffy end of my dress. I looked around for Sloan. She leaned over the counter, chatting up none other than Cowboy Joe himself.

Preston was technically a cowboy. I mean, the boy was from Texas, and according to Sloan, his jeans were so tight they deserved some form of riding, but he didn't go all out with a hat or anything. At least, not outside of Sloan's imagination.

I rolled my eyes and walked over to sit next to Ava at our usual corner booth. I threw a look over my shoulder toward Sloan and Preston. "I see I'm too late to stop her."

Sloan had purchased the knee high black leather boots she talked about, and she sported them with a black mini skirt that fit like latex over her curves. One thing was for sure...she would get his attention.

Sloan would make a blind man blush in that outfit.

Ava smiled as I slid into the booth. "If she leans any further over that counter, she's going to lick his dimples."

I held out my hand for her phone because mine was buried in the black depths of my backpack in case my dad tried to call. I didn't want to miss this prime opportunity to annoy Sloan, though. Ava instinctively knew what I wanted and shoved her phone in my hand while she scooted over so she could see what I typed.

I quickly typed out a text to Sloan.

Ava: Back away from the cowboy with your hands up.

After taking Sloan's order, for what I'm sure was

the third time in the past twenty minutes, Preston walked away, and Sloan jerked her phone out of her pocket. She made a face at me and replied.

Sloan: I am behaving myself, thank you very much!

Ava and I both let out a snort. Sloan very rarely behaved.

Ava: Tell that to the stool you're molesting.

I knew as soon as she registered it because she looked down and adjusted herself. She whipped around to face Preston as he walked back with a cup of coffee. Sloan had a distinct middle finger stuck up in our direction behind her back.

I gave her one second to start talking again before I sent my next message.

Ava: Well whatever you do, DO NOT LOOK DOWN AT HIS CROTCH.

She peeked down at her phone, but then took her eyes straight back up to Preston. "She won't do it," Ava said confidently. "She's developing a resistance to you."

I pressed my lips into a confident grin. "Oh, just wait for it."

Sure enough, two seconds later, her gaze dropped from Preston's eyes.

Ava and I busted out laughing, and Sloan threw a menacing stare over her shoulder. "She's going to kill you," Ava sniggered while giving me a much deserved high five.

"After the week I've had, death would be a welcome release."

Sloan headed back over to the table, and she slammed the coffee down in front of me. "That's the last time I'm nice enough to order you a drink."

"Yeah, because you did that out of the pure goodness of your heart." I smirked at her, grabbing my cup of caffeinated goodness.

"At least I have the nerve to talk to him." She crossed her arms over her chest and stuck her chin in the air. "At least I hump the seat in front of him and not the one across the room."

I ignored her without success. My dating record was always up for debate, especially lately. Every Friday night that I went home alone without even a number, I got a lecture the next morning. They knew me. They knew my nunhood was by choice. I wasn't a people person. Chatting with people I didn't know in a bar wasn't my cup of tea. I liked familiarity. I liked a certain kind of person. I didn't like drunk guys with the personality of tree bark asking why my shoes didn't match my dress, or how my hair ended up this particular shade of blonde. They didn't care that I started dressing this way because my father hated it. They didn't care that I was born with this cotton top and no matter how many times I tried to dye it, it only faded back out in a matter of days. They didn't care at all.

They cared about the way my double digit hips swayed when I strutted to the bar for another drink. They cared about how many of those drinks it would take before I was ready to discard said crazy dress that didn't match my shoes. Confidence wasn't the issue. I could walk in a bar and out with a guy any night of the week, but would I like him? Would my father find out and use it as another excuse to steal my dream from me?

Sloan slid in the booth across from me, so I would be forced to look at her. "Seriously, Elle, when was the last time you went out on a date?"

I shrugged. "I don't know...that Christmas bash?"

"Wait." Ava held her hands in the air. "I hate to tell you, but falling asleep in the back seat of my car and waking up three hours later to find that weird guy in our English class looking through the window at you isn't considered a date."

I kicked her beneath the table. "Look, Whorella, that was New Year's."

"She's right, Ava." Sloan pointed out. "But seriously, Elle, what's up? Do you have a rule that you can only date on holidays?"

"It's not a rule." I mumbled into my drink about their meddling. My dating life was pathetic without their reminders. I didn't want tree bark boy. Or fratastic boy. Or look-at-me-I-have-tattoos boy. I wanted *my* nerd. "It just tends to happen that way."

"It tends to happen that way because you haven't embraced your college dating goddess." Ava explained it like she was some astute scholar on my libido. "And on the holidays you finally put your books and your standards down and let yourself have fun."

"Good point." Sloan agreed too easily, which

31

meant they were about to team up on me. Sloan tapped her chin while she considered her options. "If you're going to be so intent on forgoing all the bar guys, then we have to work on your nerd issues. I think all we need to do is get our little Elle here hopped up on the magic juice and shove her in the direction of the library."

"That is the surefire way to get Elle loosened up. A shot or two of tequila and you'll talk to anyone. Even Library Boy." Ava thought about it and nodded. "Tequila shots at our next study session and the rest will take care of itself."

They sat smiling at each other like they had solved some difficult equation. I thought about screaming at them. I was in a screaming, pull some hair out, all out catfight kind of mood, but another option crossed my mind. A better, more satisfying, option. At that very moment, walking directly toward us, was Cowboy Joe. Sloan was right about at least one thing. That boy wore some tight pants.

Preston slowly walked over to our table. His soft, brown hair was combed and perfectly placed. His pressed shirt was tucked in his jeans to showcase the extra large and extra shiny belt buckle.

"Miss Sloan." He smiled down at her and then turned to Ava and me. "Ladies. Can I get you anything else?"

I grinned to myself. Sloan was predictable. Good ol' predictable Sloan. I waited until she was about to open her mouth and then I let mine drop open. "Sloan! Stop staring at his crotch. I mean, he's looking right at you."

Sloan's eyes widened. I was positive of her next

action. Her gaze was on his crotch as soon as he looked down. I leaned back in my seat and took another sip of my coffee.

Score one point for Eloise.

Sloan nearly killed me. Of course, she waited until we were safely outside, away from the still blushing Cowboy Joe. The only reason I survived was because I got a head start and there was no way she would ruin her new pair of hoochie boots to catch me.

Silly little pixie.

I stopped at the crosswalk down the street and waited for her. The wind blew her long black hair around her head like a slutty Medusa. "You'll pay for that, Duncan. You just wait. When we get to the pub tomorrow night, I will give out your number to every male in that building."

I winced, not because of her threat. It wouldn't be the first time she randomly handed my number out to strange guys. I forgot to tell them about the change in my schedule. "Yeah, about Friday nights…"

Ava immediately straightened up. "You're going with us, Elle. You promised. It's the only place outside of the baseball field where I might actually get an opportunity to run into Brad."

I shrunk down an inch. "Well, you see, I might have gotten kicked out of my normal anatomy class, and I had to get switched into a new section."

They both rounded on me. "What? How did you get kicked out?"

"It's a long story." The phone in my backpack started to buzz. It would be my dad for the third time today. A constant reminder of my never ending failures. If my dad found out I got kicked out of a class, he'd probably make me transfer mid-semester. If he found out that it was because of my obsession with Library Boy... "The point is...Friday nights at Rowdy Randy's are no longer an option for me. I have class."

Ava deflated and I somehow felt even more guilty. I tried to smile reassuringly at her. "The good news is I made enough extra money to buy season tickets to baseball. I'll be there at every game with you."

Ava's brows pinched together. "Darn right, you'll be there every game."

I placed my hands on her shoulders then gave her a quick hug. "I'm sorry, Ava. I didn't mean to screw up our plans."

She sighed. That was the thing about Ava—she was the most forgiving person on the planet. "It'll be fine."

I looked over at Sloan. She scowled at me. "I'm still giving your number out. So, I wouldn't keep my phone on in class if I were you."

I hugged her too. Sloan's shell was a little tougher than Ava's, but even the queen bee of grudges couldn't resist a bear hug. Sloan hugged me back because she knew I hated it. "I'm still mad at you," she mumbled into my hair.

"And I'm still not sorry, so it's okay."

She shoved me away from her, but she laughed. "So, where are you going now?"

"You mean after we go spend all our money on baseball tickets? I'm going to the library to study."

Ava eyed me, wiggling her eyebrow suggestively. "To actually study, or *study?*"

I smiled. "To actually study. I'll have a quiz tomorrow night in my new anatomy class. I have to be ready for it."

Sloan sighed, disappointed. "Fine. Let's go buy our tickets so you can go be smarty pants."

I curtsied. "Thank you for your kind consideration, your highness."

She knocked her elbow with mine then linked our arms together. "You're welcome."

We walked like that down the street, arms intertwined. Ava and Sloan didn't realize what their small gestures meant to me. Their friendship kept me going, even as my phone continued to buzz in my backpack. I no longer felt the panic and stress like I did before. With them by my side, I would survive. I would find a way to pass and keep this small form of independence.

I wouldn't go back home.

Ever.

Chapter Four

THE PLAN

I was going to fail anatomy. I had never, in my entire life, failed a class. I'd skipped class, bullshitted my way through a class, but never failed. In fact, I had never even made less than a B before. My afternoon study session did nothing but reveal to me exactly how big of a slacker I'd been the past couple of weeks. I felt like I was walking around with a giant flashing F over my head all day and everyone could see it. I grabbed an early dinner on campus then went back to the library for another round. This time I was on a mission. Mission impossible. Eloise Duncan was going to go to the library to actually study two times in one day. Someone alert the media.

Bypassing my usual nerd stalking spot was by the far the hardest thing I'd ever done. It was easier earlier today because in the back of my mind I knew he was never at the library right after lunch on Thursday. But Thursday afternoons…he'd be there.

He'd be sitting there in all his beautiful, nerdy, chemistry-loving goodness.

Would he have on a tie again?

A comic shirt?

Which one? Would the color match his eyes?

I paused at the stairwell to pout. Responsibility and maturity were really ruining my life. I found a small table in the corner of the basement that appeared nice and quiet. Normally, I liked quiet. Today, though, I wished silence was a real person so I could scowl at them. And maybe punch them in the throat.

There were only a couple people in the small space of the basement, all of them very low on the Eloise-type scale. There was a guy in the corner whose face you couldn't see because he was asleep behind his fort of text books, and two other guys at the couch in the corner that walked straight out of a Dungeons and Dragons game. The one on the left was an elf. I'd bet money on it.

I found a table in the corner and pulled out a three feet by three feet poster of a skeleton and taped it up on the wall next to me. I would know every major bone on this anorexic heathen before I left this spot if it killed me. I turned my chair around so I could see nothing but the poster on the wall and stared at the skeleton. Each individual bone and the elaborate and ridiculous names next to them. Two point two seconds later boredom swallowed me whole.

I was suddenly hungry, my stomach growling and roaring, and I needed to pee. I could definitely feel a distinct ache in my bladder region. It was too hot and my tights retracted tight around my hips. Images of undone chores filed through my head, and I actually considered going home to do laundry. My face fell hopelessly into my hands.

How would I ever make this interesting enough so that I would focus?

I glanced at the skeleton again, which was actually more like a menacing grimace that could have caught it on fire, and it was then I realized my problem. I still hadn't gotten over the disappointment of bypassing my usual table upstairs. Because that was the biggest distraction of all. The temptation. One peek just to see if he was there.

Inspiration hit me.

I pulled out a Sharpie from my binder and popped off the lid. I drew a pair of black glasses around the eyes of the skeleton. I leaned back and admired my artwork.

Well, at least now it was a sexy boring skeleton. That was an improvement.

My gaze narrowed at the skeleton and I concentrated.

F-I-B-U-L-A…the big one.

Ugh. It was useless. There was only one scrawny creature I cared about memorizing right now, and he was upstairs. I fell back in my seat and tried to approach this from an angle fit for a crazy person. I closed my eyes and pictured my geek god. I imagined myself stepping up to him and taking his shirt off. I ran my hand slowly and precisely down his arm.

"Humerus. Radius. Ulna."

I opened my eyes and smiled. This could work. I closed my eyes and took off his pants. "Femur. Fibula. Tibia."

Oh, yeah…this could work.

"Mom," a voice groaned from behind me, "I'm not starving. I know I can't cook, but I do know how to order food."

I spun around to inform the rude bastard that I was trying to study when my tongue got stuck in my throat. Standing behind me on a step stool, reaching up for a book, was nerd perfect. He had his cell phone to his ear and one hand stretched up above his head.

I couldn't see his face, but I could recognize that glorious backside anywhere. His Green Lantern shirt jerked up with the motion, revealing the faint sign of black boxer shorts and…abs.

Library Boy had abs? The shirt fell back down and I quickly spun back around and tried to suppress the drool at that statistical unlikelihood.

"Yes, I know I could live off cupcakes, but I'm not just eating junk food, okay?"

I turned my head to the side slightly, watching him walk back down the aisle with his new book, still chatting away. I shot a sympathetic smile back to my skeleton and shook my head. "Sorry, Bones, but he's still got you beat."

I pulled the poster down and shoved it in my book and took off down the aisle after my nerd.

James Bond didn't have anything on me. I was in complete stealth mode. I stood in the middle of the aisle pretending to look at a book as he continued to talk on the other side of the shelf.

"Okay, we are definitely not having this conversation right now. I'm okay with listening to you lecture me about by diet, but my social life is off limits."

He moved down a few feet, and I followed. His voice was cool and calm. Every word he spoke made tiny prickles pop up on my skin.

"Look, I know Dad is a Sigma alum. Trust me, in no way, form, or fashion has he ever let me forget that. I came to college to get an education. I'm not the fraternity type." He continued to growl as he listened to whatever argument his mother gave on the other end. "It would only be a distraction."

We moved dangerously close to the edge of the book shelf, so I stopped at the corner and turned my back to it. He let out an agonizing moan, and I had to hold onto the shelf for support. "I need to finish my bio homework. Can we talk about this later?"

He emerged from between the shelves, and my back instinctively jerked inward at the thought of him standing behind me. "Love you too, Mom." He laughed and I heard the phone beep off.

He breathed in a deep, heavy sigh and my ovaries dropped down to scream at my uterus.

"You would think moving away to college would make your mother realize you're capable of taking care of yourself," he mumbled to himself. "But, no, not Oliver Edwards's mom."

With that, he stalked up the stairs with his new load of books. I turned around in time to watch his black Chucks disappear up the stairwell.

Oliver.

My nerd's name was Oliver.

Oliver Nerdilicious Edwards.

I knew his name!

I grabbed my books and quickly stuffed everything down into my backpack. I wasn't studying tonight. Tonight was not a study night. I ran up the stairs and headed back to my apartment. This was cause for a celebration.

Once I made it home, I went straight to the kitchen and started slinging open cupboards and drawers looking for everything I needed. I spent the next hour and a half whipping through my kitchen like a Tasmanian Martha Stewart. Sugar, flour, and dashes of vanilla. Butter, oil, and eggs. I broke them, stirred them, and whipped them as I sang a chorus at the top of my lungs. "Oliver Edwards. His name is Oliver Edwards." My kitchen was in complete and total shambles, but in front of me sat one beautiful creation, if I had to brag on it myself.

A cupcake.

Not just any cupcake, but my famous very vanilla cupcake with homemade strawberry cheesecake icing, topped with cherry sprinkles. I couldn't tell my femur from my ass crack, but I could sure bake the hell out of some cupcakes.

I grabbed the treat and ran full throttle back to the library. When I made it to the entrance, I bent over, gasping for air. People walked by looking at me like I was a lunatic, but I didn't care.

Oliver—no, I would never stop saying his name—sat silently studying in his usual spot. I stumbled over to a seat to wait it out. I held the cupcake in my lap as I patiently waited for my heartrate to slow down. Twenty-five minutes later, I

41

was perfectly calm, and Oliver had pulled off his glasses to rub his eyes. He put the glasses back on and leaned up to stretch. I scooted up in my seat. It was almost time.

Sure enough, Oliver stood and stretched again before walking away from his desk. I leaned over to watch him fade out of sight into the hallway, leading to the bathroom. I pounced. In a matter of seven seconds I was across the room. I strategically placed the cupcake in the middle of his book and then sprinted back in my original position.

James Bond, I tell you. Eloise Duncan, international nerd stalker extraordinaire. My stomach knotted up as he returned to his seat. He noticed something was off as he approached, and he stopped a few feet from the desk, staring at his book. He cocked his head to the side and a small smile spread across his face.

Oh. That smile.

He moved closer. He studied it a moment before finally picking it up to inspect it. He turned it around, taking a quick whiff of the icing.

Eat it. Just freaking eat it. Please, eat it.

He did something even better. He stuck his tongue out and licked the icing.

His eyes lit up with recognition. The next thing I knew, Oliver had the wrapper off and half of it in his mouth. He closed his eyes, savoring the flavor.

I squealed.

Loudly.

People around me turned and stared. "He's eating my cupcake," I said to the boy behind me who scowled in my direction. "*My* cupcake."

42

Oliver licked the icing off his fingers. I had to sit down. The table, my life support to keep my heart off the floor. He looked around the room, curious. I moved back out of sight even more than I already was, but I couldn't stop smiling.

Oliver liked my cupcakes.

He leaned back in his seat and smiled again before shaking his head. His attention went back down to his book.

I fell into the seat beside me with a thud. This library officially became my very own fantasy land. It was Walt Disney World. The place dreams came to get hot and bothered. I didn't want to leave this spot. I couldn't.

Yes, it was official. I would fail anatomy.

Chapter Five

BASEBALL

Ava straightened her perfect beauty queen ponytail before adjusting the low-cut shirt she wore into perfect position. "What do you mean, you baked him a cupcake? Please tell me that is your new slang for rocking that geek's socks off behind the poetry section."

I sighed, looking up at the clouds that floated effortless above my head. We'd been sitting in the outfield at the Maryland baseball team's first home game for thirty minutes, and I was already bored out of my mind. Said boredom was the only reason I broke down and told my friends about how I finally figured out Oliver's name. I assured myself that boredom was a legitimate excuse. If not for the sheer lack of stimuli eating me alive, I would have never admitted to my ridiculous cupcake scheme.

"No. I mean it literally. I baked the boy a cupcake." I thought about it for a second, remembering Oliver's smile and his tongue as he tested the icing. "He liked it, and I *liked* that he liked it."

Sloan glanced over at me out of the corner of her eye, her lips pursed. "He liked it? Did he tell you that?"

I stared down at the big red bows on the tips of my shoes. I patted them against the seat in front of me with a light *tip tap* sound, avoiding her question. A slow smile spread across Sloan's face. She was such a wicked pixie. "He doesn't know you're the one who baked it for him, does he?"

Maybe I was wrong the other day at the café. Maybe I was the one who was predictable.

I looked down and played with the hem of my polka-dotted dress. "Technically?"

Sloan burst out laughing, and I begrudgingly stuffed another handful of popcorn in my mouth, sinking down in my seat a little further.

"I think it was good thinking on Elle's part." Ava craned her head to get a better view of the players coming out on the field. "A man will follow his stomach anywhere most of the time. She could probably leave him a trail of cupcakes straight to her bed now."

I pointed to Ava in order to suggest she had a good point, but I couldn't help but laugh at her in the process. I sat bundled up in a jacket over my dress, the spring weather not quite cooperative for much else, while sex-on-a-stick Ava looked like she was going to the beach for spring break.

"Ava, you do realize Brad plays short stop and there is no possible way he is going to see you all the way out here?"

She slung her mane of blonde hair around in my face. "Look, Eloise. You bake your nerd cupcakes, and I'll flaunt my hoo-has to my jock. We work with what we've got."

"Would you two focus?" Sloan stole a hand full of popcorn from my box. "We're discussing Elle's first contact with Library Boy. I mean, the guy ate your freaking cupcake. You've got to introduce yourself now."

"Don't say it like that." I wrinkled my nose, my heart forming a giant lump in my throat. "You make it sound dirty."

"Sloan can make the Easter bunny X-rated," Ava said with a smile. "Besides, you said it yourself...you liked it when he ate it."

This conversation was going downhill, and downhill fast. "Did he use his tongue?" Sloan asked, intrigued. "Did he lick it nice and slow?"

Ava giggled. "Was he completely satisfied?"

There was no escaping those two once they got started. "He ate it really fast, and yes, he looked pretty damn satisfied." I crossed my arms over my chest and glared at them.

They both smirked at me in triumph. It was their goal in life to pull me down in the gutter with them. I waited because there had to be more. It was Sloan, so of course there was more. She sat up in her seat, turning all the way around to face me. "Seriously, though, this boy just ate a cupcake he found sitting on his desk? You could have laced it with the date rape drug, for all he knew."

"He apparently has a thing for cupcakes. Especially *my* cupcakes. Gretchen said he comes in

Sugar Cube once a week." I smiled at the thought. No, my internal ballerina danced a jig in my gut at the thought. "I think he recognized my icing. He couldn't resist after that."

Sloan put her hand on my shoulder. "Then why don't you rub some icing on your mouth and tell him you have a new flavor for him to try?"

Ava snorted as she eyed her man warming up over in the left field corner.

I rolled my eyes at both of them. "Or I could just bake him more and keep secretly leaving them for him to find."

"Said the crazy stalker." Sloan smirked, nudging my side.

I groaned. They didn't understand. Every time I looked at Oliver or heard his voice, I lost all ability to function. I wanted nothing more than to peel every inch of clothing off him with my teeth. If he were some normal guy, I would have already accomplished that goal. He wasn't normal, though. He was Oliver Edwards.

Ava kicked me, and I realized Brad Helton, with all two hundred and fifty pounds of muscle in tow, was headed our direction, smiling like a breastfed baby at the Playboy mansion.

"Hello, ladies." His voice boomed from the field beneath our seats, and Ava leaned over the rail, giving him a perfect view of her barely-there shirt.

"Hello." Ava stated it as if she were completely bored out of her mind.

I officially hated her. Out of the people at the game, Brad had not only spotted her, but decided to trot over for a friendly chat?

The world was cruel. Evil, nerd-deprivingly cruel.

It depressed me that I was being forced to witness this exchange of sexual Jedi mind games. Neither of them took the tact to be mysterious or unobvious. Brad might as well have waved his hand in front of her face and said, "Show me the hoohas," while Ava repeated the same gesture instructing, "I wanna see nothing but cleats." Brad never took his eyes off Ava's chest, and Ava was about to sling herself over the railing on top of him. I grabbed the edge of her scanty shirttail just to be safe.

My only saving grace was when the coach finally yelled for them to come to the dugout, and Brad was forced to unlock his gaze from the Holy Grails. Then, of course, Ava was so high on pheromones that you couldn't understand a word that came out of her mouth. She kept mumbling about chocolate syrup, chains, and Barry White.

Either way, I was jealous. Both Sloan and Ava were well on their way to apprehending their fantasy boys, while I watched from the sidelines. I wasn't overtly confident like Sloan or physically gratifying like Ava. I was determined to work with what I had.

Cupcakes.

After the baseball game, I went to the grocery store, and I'm not going to lie…I went a little crazy with the cupcake supplies. Should I have been studying instead?

You betcha.

Should I have finally answered one of the ten voicemails my dad left me?

Probably.

I managed a high C on my quiz Friday, but it wouldn't be enough to jerk my grade up. I had an itch, though. It had to be scratched. I had to provide Oliver with more cupcakes. I put my heart and soul into those recipes. I wanted to watch him enjoy them.

I taped a different page from my recipe book on the fridge for every day of the upcoming week. I put on my favorite Betty Boop apron and twirled around my kitchen like a flour fairy.

Monday, I left Oliver a dazzling display of chocolate and chocolate with strawberry sprinkles. He looked around the room suspiciously before devouring it in a matter of seconds. The chocolate smeared over his lips as he licked it off, and I died a little inside. Okay, so maybe died was the wrong verb, but it was less embarrassing.

Tuesday, I got a little creative with chocolate chip and butter cream icing. I could have sworn he eyed his desk as soon as he came back around the corner from retrieving a book. It made the smile on his face when he saw it sitting there even sweeter.

Wednesday, bravery struck me and I drew a smiley face on the top, complete with black glasses. He crinkled his nose up as he examined my sugary artwork, and then he let out a laugh while he bit his lip. Yes, a laugh. A laugh that I had induced.

Thursday, I showed up early hoping to get some actual studying done before he arrived because, let's face it. After he arrived, I didn't care if I ended up a hobo on the street singing *Thriller* for pennies as long he moaned when he licked my cupcake. I finally decided to give myself a little quiz to see exactly how much I knew for this week's quiz.

Bad idea.

I sat there with my foot hooked around the leg of the chair and wept on the list of terms that would be my downfall. I knew how to spell the names of the bones, and I could think of about thirty different ones, but I couldn't remember which one was which. Unfortunately, that was kind of the whole point. I slammed the book shut and shoved it off the desk into my backpack with the feeling of complete doom washing over me. After I gave Oliver his cupcake, I snuck off to go in to work early. I needed to carve out some actual study time or I would end up back in Hollyhell for good.

I hurried through the orders Gretchen set out for me, and it helped lighten my mood. People were requesting my cupcakes for special events. Three different birthday parties wanted two dozen of my double chocolate everythings. I prepped another batch and put them in the oven. The doorbell dinged, and I heard Gretchen greet the customer as I closed the oven and set the timer.

"Surprise. Surprise. I'm back."

This time I recognized the voice immediately.

My back snapped straight. I'd given Oliver a cupcake not even two hours ago, and he was already back in the shop? That boy had a cupcake addiction. No wonder I liked him so much.

"Nice to see you again," Gretchen said. "What can I get you?"

There was a long pause, and I could imagine him silently eyeing the cupcake case. "Well, actually,

I'm not here to buy anything. I was kind of hoping to ask you a question."

"Sure. What's up?"

I ran to the door to eavesdrop. The side of Oliver's face was barely visible above the counter. His hair defied gravity today. There didn't seem to be any mousse or some other kind of anything added to it. It just naturally stood up on the ends in this super sexy, nonchalant way. "Someone seems to have figured out my not-so-secret obsession with the cupcakes from your shop."

That perked Gretchen up. Her eyes lit up like Christmas lights.

Crap. Oliver was totally going to out me to my boss.

Gretchen tapped her fingers across the cash register. "Oh, really?"

"Yeah. Someone keeps leaving them on my desk at the library every time I leave. I was just wondering." He pointed at the sign above the cupcake case with my name on it. "This Eloise...she's an eighty-year-old woman, right? Gray hair. Apron with giant apples on it."

Gretchen's grin got so big it revealed every tooth in her mouth. "Do you think Eloise is giving you the cupcakes?"

Oliver blushed. "I know it sounds crazy."

"No. Not crazy at all. Whoever this person is, though...they must really be smitten with you to go through so much trouble." You could hear the teasing in Gretchen's voice. She knew it was me. Of course, she freaking knew it was me.

Again, Oliver's blush only deepened. As if he

51

wasn't cute enough already.

Gretchen tapped her fingers along the top of the counter, now moving slowly toward me. "To answer your question, Eloise is definitely not eighty years old. However, I should also point out that she's sold close to two hundred cupcakes this week. A lot of them to pretty young girls."

Oliver tried to smile, but he only ended up awkwardly shoving his hands in his pockets. "Thanks for the info." He started to back away toward the door, but then stopped when he put his hand on the glass. "Next time you see Eloise...tell her I really do like her cupcakes."

Gretchen glanced toward the kitchen door. "Will do."

The doorbell dinged again, and I ran back to my station and started stirring random ingredients together which turned out to be sugar and more sugar. Oliver caused my brain to dysfunction. Something about him caused the wires to get crossed and my hormones to go haywire. Gretchen rounded the corner and laughed at the sight of me. "Oh, don't you dare stand there and act like you weren't listening. I could see your face in the reflection of the glass."

I looked guilty. So terribly guilty. I shrugged and continued to stir my sugar concoction. "I may have overheard the conversation."

Gretchen laughed again as she leaned against the doorframe, a smug grin forming on her face. "You've been leaving him the cupcakes, haven't you?"

"I don't know." I scraped the tiled floor with the

toe of my shiny, canary yellow shoes. "Would that make me crazy and desperate?"

"Only if it didn't work. Seems to me like your little plan is working out quite well for you."

I frowned down at the bowl. "Maybe."

"What do you mean? He made a trip all the way down here to ask about you. He wants it to be you."

I bit my lip. "You don't know how much I like the fact that he likes what I do. Baking...it's my life."

"Then go tell him. Introduce yourself."

I stirred the sugar around in the bowl again. "It isn't that simple."

Gretchen walked over, her fingers tilting my chin up. "It is that simple, Eloise. Look at you...you're a catch. That boy would be putty in your hands. Heck, he practically is already, and he doesn't even know it's you yet."

The grin was too strong to deny. It sounded too easy, though. Too perfect. Happy endings weren't exactly my thing. I'd always been a "watch the world from the sideline" kind of girl. I daydreamed behind the safety of my mixing bowl. This game I played with Oliver started to feel too real. Or maybe it already was real, and I was too scared to lose it. I always lost everything I cared about. My father made sure of it. He pushed my mother away, he ran off every friend I ever cared about and dating wasn't an option. Boys weren't part of the detailed plan he had for my life.

Gretchen wrapped her arm around my shoulder. "Tell him, Eloise. You owe it to yourself to give it a shot."

Suddenly, my canary heels felt sweaty. "I'll consider it."

And I would. Unfortunately for me, though, I already knew what my answer would be. It would take something stronger than a pep talk to get this girl in the game. An Oliver-shaped bulldozer, perhaps?

Chapter Six

BOOKS

The next week, I spent my every waking hour studying in between classes and work. I had a project due in history and a paper to finish in English, on top of my extra study efforts with anatomy. Floundering sounded like an appropriate word to describe my week. Surviving as I flailed around aimlessly, barely managing to keep my head above water. I could feel my mental efforts weakening. I would drown soon, and before I knew it, I would wake up in California Dad-controlled hell.

The coffee I practically pumped into my system like lifeblood gave me the jitters. My knee bounced wildly under the table as I tapped my pencil against the spine of my book. A diagram and a list of terms sat in front of me, but my eyes were directed across the room.

Oliver was in the library. It was Wednesday. Oliver wasn't supposed to be in the library on

Wednesday. Yes, I had a box of cupcakes in my bag. They were extras I planned to share with Sloan and Ava later, but now I felt obligated to give one to Oliver. It was a new recipe I wanted my friends to taste test before I tried it at the shop, but my nerd would do just as well. If Oliver liked it, I really didn't care if anyone else liked it.

He'd only been at his usual spot for a couple minutes, so I knew he wouldn't take a break anytime soon. He disappeared to go make a copy of something at the station behind me, so I tried to use the free time to concentrate on my own work. These new terms that professor gave us for the week were even more confusing than last week. Why was it required to memorize every tiny notch and dent on your face? You couldn't even see those notches on a real person. So, why did it matter?

I got the inferior nasal concha mixed up with the palatine bone for the third time, and it was all I could take. I slammed the book shut and shoved it off the table. Maybe the library floor would open up and a giant bookworm would eat it and go regurgitate it in Dr. Howard's face.

A loud grunt echoed beside me as my book crashed to the floor. I tilted my head up. Oliver stared down at me, pain flashing through his eyes. His right hand cupped itself over his crotch and he let out a small whine before dropping down to his knees.

I sucked in a breath of air as my fingers clamped around the edge of the desk.

Oh, crap.

I did not just do that.

No. No. No.

I *did not* hit Oliver in the nuts with a ten-pound book.

Another groan ripped out of him and his left hand tangled itself in his hair. I wanted to talk. I needed to talk. I had to talk to him, but I couldn't. I couldn't get words to come out of my mouth. My mouth moved, shaking, grasping for functionality, but failing. I stood and bent over him, freaking the hell out, but still unable to form words. He groaned again and looked up, his blue eyes locking onto mine.

Pain. It flickered outward, pleading for help. What could I do? What would I do? I had just broken what I assumed would be my most favorite part of the guy who consumed my every fantasy. What did I say after something like that?

"Sorry," I finally managed to blurt out, but his gaze dropped back to the floor as he cupped his other hand over himself. He fell forward almost involuntarily. "Shit."

My hands swirled around in front of me, not sure what to do. Should I touch him? Help him up?

He moaned again. This time louder, more painful.

"I really am so sorry."

He shifted in an attempt to stand, but it only resulted in another agonizing moan. "Tell that to my balls when you find them," he mumbled, and my entire world shattered around me.

He wasn't just angry with me. He was pissed. Well, no crap. I introduced a textbook to his precious gems by unmerciful means of force. Did I expect him to be thrilled about it?

"What the heck was that?" He groaned again, looking behind him at my book.

I sucked in a breath, trying to keep myself calm. "Introduction to Anatomy."

He snorted and shook his head. "Sounds about right."

He panted out a few breaths that made my heart stutter in uneven beats, and then he held his hand out to me. "A little help?"

I stared at the hand. He wanted me to touch him. He wanted me to touch his hand that seconds before had been cupping his balls.

I grabbed him as he slowly moved himself up to his feet, making unfavorable grimaces the whole time. Once standing, he released my hold and reached for the table. He gently sat on the edge with a small whine escaping his lips.

I took a few steadying breaths myself. I'd probably maimed him for life. That was what I would be known for from now on. Not my cupcakes. I would be the girl who broke the beautiful nerd.

"Next time you decide to go Carrie on your textbook, do a one-two check on either side...'kay?"

I couldn't help but let out a slight giggle as he bent down, obviously testing his range of motion before sitting himself back up on the table.

"Will do." Geez, I felt horrible. This was not how I wanted our first introduction go. Not that I planned for there to be an actual introduction, but if I dared to dream about it, this wouldn't have been it.

I nervously tucked my hair behind my ear. "I really am sorry. I was frustrated. I honestly would never do that to a guy on purpose."

He nodded as his gaze ran over the floor toward my book. "Frustrated, huh? Anatomy can be tough."

I rolled my eyes. "It's kicking my butt." Because of him, but I let that part slide. "I'm kind of failing right now."

He studied me for a moment, and I suddenly got extremely self-conscious. I admitted to the boy who studies for a living that I'm failing a class. Probably not the best way to impress him.

Oliver didn't appear disgusted by my confession, though. Instead, he eyed my dress. It was red today, with tiny blue birds printed over every visible inch of it. The V-neck was low and my cleavage louder than the quirky pattern. He tried to glance over it back to my face. Tried and failed. Miserably.

"I've seen you around," he said, clearing his throat and finally locking his eyes back on mine. "A lot, actually. You sit here at this desk most of time, right?"

He noticed me?

Oh, my gosh. He noticed me. And not just the two times I'd made a fool out of myself.

I nodded. It wouldn't be smart for me to talk right now.

"You come in with two other girls sometimes too. A little one and the one that wears all the pink?"

Again, I nodded.

He glanced back at the stack of books on my desk. "You study almost as much as me, but you're still failing?"

Stalking and studying were two totally different things, but I didn't think he needed an explanation. "That subject seems to be my weak link." Anatomy, along with his glasses, his pants, and every other nerdy little thing about him.

He stood from the desk, cautiously adjusting himself. "Would you like some help?"

"Help?" I squeaked as he pushed his glasses up his nose.

"Yeah. Well, on behalf of all innocent college guys everywhere, I feel kind of obligated to help you relieve this frustration of yours before you attack again." He smiled. It was a gorgeous, slow smile that only he could make look seductive and kind at the same time. "I could help you with your anatomy."

I bet he could.

Random sounds that weren't English came out of my mouth before I managed to shut it again.

We stood there, looking at each other, and he raised an eyebrow. "Is that a yes? Or a 'no, freaky boy, get your bruised nuts away from me'?"

"Uhh...um...uhh." Crap, there I went again. I ran a hand through my tussled hair as I tried to rein in my nerves. "The first one."

He laughed and crossed his arms. "Well, grab your torture device there and join me over at my desk."

I nodded.

In fact, I nodded ten times before I could make myself stop and actually pick up all my books. He smiled, and I followed him over to his desk, checking out his ass the entire time.

Knocking guys in the crotch with a book was apparently a new perfectly acceptable introduction technique. *Boys everywhere, hide in fear.*

I sat in the chair next to him, letting my backpack slide from my arm. He cleaned off the desk to make room for my books. My hand slowly reached out in a mock effort to squeeze his ass, but I quickly repositioned myself as he sat.

Reflexes like a cat, I have. A horny, "hump your leg off like a Rottweiler" cat.

He turned to face me, and I propped my chin in my hand and smiled. I was in heaven.

"I'm Oliver, by the way. Oliver Edwards." He linked his hands in front of him on the desk. "I guess I kind of forgot to mention that before."

At the thought of it, his hand reflexively moved over his crotch. I would have to make up for my accident somehow.

"You were a little occupied." I tried to smile politely, but then I panicked. I couldn't tell him I was Eloise. What if he instantly put two and two together? He saw me here at the library, and my name also happened to be the same as the girl who made his favorite cupcakes. He would know. "I'm Elle. Elle Duncan."

Even with the use of my nickname, I waited to see his reaction. He nodded and scooted his chair closer to the desk, and I scooted mine closer to him. "So, you're having trouble with anatomy?"

He ran his fingers through his hair, and I realized he was waiting for me to answer. "Uhh, yeah...trouble with anatomy."

61

My gaze dropped to his crotch, and I mentally kicked myself. I was not turning into Sloan today.

"So, what are you having trouble with, exactly?"

He had the absolute cutest serious expression ever. I had no idea how I thought I would survive this without embarrassing myself. I already wanted to poke him to make sure he was real.

"Bones." *Do not look down...do not look down. You are not Sloan.* "The bones and everything on the facial skeleton are giving me a hard time."

He nodded as I focused my attention on the glasses. "I guess they are pretty easy to get mixed up. We could try making up some kind of saying with the first letter of each name that would help you remember."

"You mean like pretty savory cake?"

His eyes widened and I stifled a giggle.

"You know like pelvis, sacrum, coccyx," I explained further, "have some cake. That's how I managed to pass last week's quiz."

"Oh. Uh, yeah. Kind of like that."

Note to self—nerdy boy blushes easily.

I liked.

"How about we split the face up into sections and write out the list of bones in that portion, and then we can come up with some stuff?"

I smiled and nodded like a clueless bobble-head.

I studied a lot that next hour. None of it had anything to do with anatomy. I studied the way Oliver held his pencil. He had an awkward grip, like he held the pencil too tight. His writing was small and precise. The complete opposite of my large, looping cursive. I also studied the way his lips moved when he read, and how his eyelashes fluttered when he looked up at me through his glasses.

I knew Oliver better than any textbook. I even studied his things. His black on black backpack had a silver batman keychain attached to the zipper. His notebook had a cartoon depiction of the solar system on it. He had a to-do list pinned to the top of it.

1. **Finish chem lab questions**
2. **Mail out Dex's new X-Men figurine**
3. **History project group meeting (Annex bld 4:00)**
4. **Dinner***
5. **Finish English paper**

I scooted a little closer, eyeing the star next to the word *dinner* on his list. He noticed me staring. I pointed my pen at the note. "What's with the star?"

He bit the inside of his jaw, tapping his pencil against the table. "Ah. It's nothing. Sometimes my dinner schedule gets messed up." He pointed at my book. "Are you ready for your first quiz?"

I glared at him. "A quiz? You mean, like, right now?"

He smiled like the thought of a test actually brought him joy. "Yeah. How else are we going to know if you know it yet?"

I held up my hands. "Wait a second. I'm not finished with my questions yet." I pointed back at the paper. "Who is Dex?"

He glanced at the paper again, a small smile

developing on his lips. "My little brother. His birthday is next week."

"And he likes X-Men?"

He beamed with pride. "Well, yeah, doesn't every ten-year-old boy like X-Men?"

I grinned at him. This was absolutely perfect. "What would he do if instead of a figurine, you sent him an *X-Men Origins: Wolverine* poster signed by Hugh Jackman?"

Oliver's eyes widened. "He'd pee his little X-Men loving pants."

I pulled my shoulders back, proud. "Awesome. It could use a good home."

Oliver scratched his head. "You have this poster?"

I nodded. "And before you ask, yes, I am very much willing to part with it. I'm from Hollywood. I lived not too far from the theater where they hold a lot of the big movie premieres. Sometimes I would go and wait in line and get celebrity autographs."

Oliver slid up in his seat, instantly intrigued. "Wow. That's really cool. You have anyone else I'd know?"

I'd hoped he'd ask. I pointed at the white writing on the black t-shirt he wore under his jacket. I read the quote out loud. "The blood sucking Brady Bunch. That's a quote from *The Lost Boys*, right?"

The Lost Boys was an eighties vampire movie that I probably watched at least a thousand times in my childhood.

He pulled his jacket apart and stared down at his shirt. "It was one of my favorite movies as a kid."

"I got Kiefer Sutherland's autograph."

"You're kidding."

"I didn't stand in line for it, though. I ran into him at the Starbucks in West Hills one day. I totally fangirled on him and called him Doc Spurlock. You know...from *Young Guns*?"

Oliver laughed. "I remember him as Doc. That's one of my favorite movies too."

We sat there and smiled at each other, my heart pounding in my chest. It was like I had word vomit. It was totally out of character for me. I didn't normally like talking to new people, but maybe it was because Oliver wasn't new. He'd become familiar to me. Or maybe it was the t-shirt. If there was one thing I knew, it was old occult movies and books.

Oliver leaned over the desk closer to me. "So, what did he sign for you?"

I smiled a brilliant smile. "My high school yearbook. It was the only thing I had with me at the time."

He leaned back in his seat, impressed. "Suddenly my yearbook sounds so boring."

"Sometimes it pays to be in the right place at the right time." And knock someone in the nuts.

"But you know what else I noticed? You just did a really awesome job of diverting my attention away from your test."

I grinned. "Noticed that, did ya?"

"If you're not ready, it's okay. When is your actual test?"

I let out a huff at the thought. "Friday night."

"I'm usually here on Thursday afternoons, if you want to come by tomorrow and take your pre-test then?"

My toes clenched in my shoes as I tried to keep a straight face. "Is that a date?"

It came out. Like, the question literally fell out of my mouth. I tried to stop it. I even held my hands out so the words had somewhere to land. I tried to backtrack. "Like a study date. You sitting there. Me here. Studying at the same place."

Oliver's gaze scanned the books in front of him. He couldn't even look at me as the shy smile captured his features. "Yeah. A study date."

I swallowed, and it sounded more like a very loud gulp. "Okay. I'll bring your brother that poster, if you think he'd like it."

Finally, he looked up. "Yeah. He would love it."

"Okay."

Oliver intertwined his fingers. "Okay."

Awkward turtles we were…both of us. It was awesome. He rubbed the back of his neck. "Well, I still need to finish my chem lab questions."

I waved my hands over my list of terms. "I still need to study some more."

We both smiled, and no one moved. We silently went to our books, no more words spoken between us. None were needed. We sat there like that, working independently next to each other. We'd share a smile, or a random glance, but that was it. It was comfortable. Familiar. It was everything I hoped being with Oliver Edwards would be. Minus the whole maiming his genitals thing.

Chapter Seven

A NEW THING

The evening rush at Sugar Cube was chaotic. I hurried to refill the case out front with a new batch of cupcakes after a lady came in and bought out what was left for her daughter's slumber party. Sloan held the door to the case open for me as I shoved myself inside it to arrange each one perfectly. I must have been taking too long because Sloan's face peeked around the corner. "So, are you going to tell me what the super, big emergency is?"

I glanced over my shoulder at her then refocused on rotating the cupcakes so their best side showed to the public. "I told you we have to wait for Ava to get here first."

Sloan huffed impatiently. "And you're positive this news can't wait until after your shift tonight?"

"No. Definitely not."

Sloan leaned up against the side of the case as I wiggled my way back out and carefully shut the door. Sloan grabbed the edge of my apron and twisted it around her fingers. "Just tell me. Now. Please."

I pulled my apron free of her grasp and started back to the kitchen. Ava should arrive any minute, and I didn't want to have to tell the story twice. "Be patient," I said over my shoulder.

Gretchen grabbed Sloan on her way into the kitchen behind me. "After she tells you, come tell me. I want to know why she came in here skipping like Mary Sunshine today."

"Skipping isn't a crime," I yelled from around the corner.

Sloan stepped into view, watching me as I started the giant mixer and added ingredients. When I turned back around, Sloan crossed her arms over her chest, a sly smile forming on her lips. "Are you dancing?"

"What? No. I am certainly not dancing."

"Yes, you were. Your tush was shaking it." She stepped closer, her gaze honed in on my blushing face. "Did you talk to him?"

"Who?"

"You know exactly who. You talked to him today, didn't you?"

Do not smile. Do not smile.

"No."

Sloan's eyes practically popped out of her head. "Liar."

I winced and Sloan pounced on me. "Holy crap! Eloise…"

Sloan shook my body like I was a piggy bank with one dime left. I grabbed hold of her forearms to try to stabilize myself, but she started shaking

68

along with me. "How did this happen? Did he approach you? Oh my gosh, did you approach him?"

Unraveling myself from her grasp, I quickly darted around the side of the counter to safety. "Well...something like that."

"What do you mean?"

I bit my lip and peeked around the door to make sure Gretchen wasn't in hearing range. "I mean, I sort of made the initial...contact."

"Contact? Are you an alien mothership now? Just tell me what the hell happened."

I must have made an awkward, possibly pathetic face, because Sloan lost all excitement. "Elle?"

"I was studying," I said quickly, because I had to either get it out fast or not at all. "I didn't see him walking by and I kind of shoved my big anatomy textbook off the table in frustration."

Her brows creased. "And?"

"And it might have gone directly into his crotch."

Sloan paused. As in air flow ceased from her body. She closed her eyes. "I'm sorry. I don't think I heard you correctly. I thought you said you hit him in the crotch with your anatomy book."

I winced. "I did. It was horrible."

Sloan leaned across the table. "Is he okay? Did it hurt him?"

"He was definitely down for the count for a couple solid minutes. But I think everything survived."

Her fingers splayed across her face. "Only you, Elle Duncan."

"I know," I said, almost whining out the words. "But it did lead to a conversation. Then that conversation led to us sitting together to study. And now he wants to meet again tomorrow to help me study for my quiz on Friday."

Sloan grabbed her heart. "You have a date?"

The goofiest smile erupted on my face. "A study date, but yeah."

Now both hands clutched her chest and she feigned a heart attack. I grabbed a handful of flour out of the bowl on the table and threw it at her. "You don't have to act so damn surprised."

Sloan laughed, her smile vibrant as she bounced around the counter to me. "I'm so proud of you. So, what did he think about you leaving him the cupcakes? Was he surprised?"

I inched back a step. I nodded slightly and hummed something under my breath that wasn't exactly English and tried to play it off. "So, you have to help me figure out what to wear tomorrow. Okay?"

Sloan's hand clenched tight against her hip that already cocked out to the side. "Eloise," she said curtly. "You did not answer my question."

I forced out a smile. "I'm thinking something classic. Black and red, perhaps?"

Her eyes narrowed. "Why didn't you tell him you're the one who left him the cupcakes?"

I deflated against the counter. I should have known better than to think I could conveniently skip over that part. Sloan was a truth seeking shark, and her bite more naggy than painful. "It didn't seem pertinent to the conversation at the time."

"Not pertinent? Elle, you can't possibly believe—"

I held up my hands. "Stop. I can't. Not yet."

Sloan gave me the most pathetic look imaginable. And I'm sure I returned it. "Sweetie," she said, her voice all motherly now, "you can't not tell him it was you. When he finds out where you work...what your name is...he'll know."

"Those are all very rational facts."

Sloan pressed her lips together. She knew me. Rational wasn't a realistic expectation. "Soon," she said, finally. "Promise me."

I nodded and she flung herself at me. Her python-like hug engulfed me from all angles. "I love you, Eloise Duncan. And I really am proud of you."

"Yeah. Yeah." I tried to push her off, but she wasn't willing to let go. Instead, she squeezed me tighter.

"And for the record. You should totally do red and black tomorrow."

Finally, I hugged her back. "Thanks."

Over Sloan's shoulder, Gretchen stood in the doorway of the kitchen, her fingers pressed over her mouth as if she might cry. "I'm proud of you too."

Rolling my eyes, I motioned her over to join our sap-fest. All I did was talk to the guy. You would think I performed some massive feat of heroism. Maybe lost a limb and saved a few orphans. As their hugs pressed tighter against me, I realized that maybe my making the first move, even though unintentionally, really was something to be proud about. At least in my own tiny bubble of personal

71

accomplishments. For the first time…maybe ever, I was sincerely proud of myself too.

And then my phone buzzed in my backpack. My body stiffened. All sense of accomplishment and flush of self-esteem crashed and burned at my feet. It was like he knew. A sixth sense that told my father the right time to dash my dreams and damper any inkling of pride in myself. I glanced over my shoulder at my bag. I wanted to answer it. It was a horrible habit. Or maybe it was something deeper and much worse than a habit. Fear?

Was I actually scared of him?

I told myself constantly that it was merely his financial support I couldn't survive without, but broke kids went to college all the time. Something else kept that cord I couldn't break bound between us. And in this moment, as the buzzing continued in the background, that small jab in my stomach told me everything I needed to know about my relationship with my father.

I didn't know what he would do if I left him too. And I was scared to find out.

Gretchen leaned back. "Is that your phone?"

"Umm. No. It's fine. Probably just Ava, anyway."

My voice shook, and Sloan noticed immediately. Her hand remained on my back. She knew my father. She'd met him once. He'd looked down his nose at her, as if deciding in the moment it took her to introduce herself that he didn't like her. Maybe it was her confidence. Her girl power, rule the world attitude. Whatever it was, my father had made it clear we weren't to be friends.

I asked her to hang out as soon as he left and we'd been friends ever since. Sloan didn't ask too many questions about my father, but she knew. She was excellent at reading me. Just like now. She rubbed my shoulder. If Gretchen wasn't there, she would tell me it would be okay. To ignore him. To let the cord fray and break for good. Even though I wanted out, it was difficult to imagine my life without him. It was all I knew. And the unknown was scary too.

I tucked my hair behind my ears and blew out a nervous breath. Defying him made me sick to my stomach. Something as simple as ignoring his calls kept me on edge. I needed to do something to get my mind off it, or I would call him back. And I was certain if I admitted the truth to him, that would be the end of it. No more college in Maryland. No more friends he didn't pre-approve. No more freedom. And definitely no more Oliver.

"I really need to get these cupcakes in the oven," I said, easing myself away from Sloan and Gretchen in my usual "distance myself from everything good" kind of way.

The look on Gretchen's face told me she thought my sudden change in demeanor was fishy, but she didn't push it. "Well, let me know if you need anything."

I smiled politely. "Of course."

Sloan waited silently until she left and she kissed the side of my head. "You are strong, my sweet Elle. You keep doing what is best for you. I'm here if you need me."

Now my smile was fake. "Thanks. Do you think

73

you could call Ava and tell her the story? I really need to be alone and bake for a while."

"Sure. But call me tomorrow after your date, okay?"

"Absolutely. Celebration pie at my place?"

"Oh, you know me so well," she said, humming a moan of pleasure at the thought of my homemade pie.

Sloan gave me a quick hug then disappeared out the back door, leaving me to my silent refuge. I closed my eyes and took in the soft, buttery smell of my cupcake mix, perfectly blended, waiting for me in the mixer.

"I can do this," I said to myself.

I could talk to Oliver Edwards.

I could make myself proud, because that was the only opinion that truly mattered.

***

Who knew that "get your beauty sleep" was a literal thing? After another sleepless, nightmare filled night, my hair looked like something from a Gwen Stefani video. It defied gravity and reason. Maybe I walked in my sleep through my apartment and stuck my finger in a socket without realizing it. I attempted to maneuver a comb through it, but it only made it angry and ultimately frizzier. I texted for backup from the only person I knew who could save me.

Eloise: 911

Eloise: S.O.S

Eloise: Code Crazy Frizz.

Ava: How bad are we talking about? Should I bring my Frizz Be Gone?

Eloise: It's bring a wig bad. HELP!

Ava: On my way. Be there in 10.

I sat in front of my mirror, my face cupped in my hands, the comb entangled and lost amid the rabid, snapping follicles of my hair. This was so bad. I couldn't go meet Oliver looking like Frankenstein's girlfriend. I whined into my hands, hoping I would somehow wake up to realize it was another horrible dream. I didn't wake, but Ava did keep true to her word and knocked on my door before her ten-minute time limit expired. I jerked the door open, and Ava almost dropped the bag of hair supplies at the sight of me. "Whoa."

I frowned at her. "Thanks for the confidence boost."

She came inside, and I shut the door. "I'm sorry," she said, reaching up to touch the trapped comb, "but normally you're all quirky vixen-like with your little Marilyn Monroe curls. But this—" She pulled her hand away as if my hair might actually bite.

"Yes. I get it. It's scary. Can we please fix this before my study date with Oliver?"

Ava's smile burst onto her face. "I still can't

believe you have a date."

I rolled my eyes as I stomped off into my bathroom. "Yes. Eloise has a date. Everyone is so surprised and fascinated. We should take pictures and document it, so future generations will believe you when you tell how you witnessed it firsthand."

Ava gave my elbow a playful shove. "Oh, don't be a grouch. Just because your hair has performed a coup doesn't mean you have to be a smartass."

I crossed my arms over my chest. "I don't have to be one. I just want to be."

Ava directed me over to the edge of my bed where she sat me down on the floor. She took the position behind me on the bed and started trying to free my comb from captivity. I winced every time she pulled a strand. My hair was always so sensitive. It knew just how to torture me. "So, what are you going to wear?"

I pointed toward the closet door to the little black dress hanging from the doorknob. "That?"

"Yeah. Why? What's wrong with it?"

"It's nice," Ava said in the same patronizing tone one might use to describe the boy your grandmother always wanted you to date. "It's just not what I had in mind for you."

I tried to crane my head back so I could look at her. Or rather, glare. "If you think I'm showing up at the library dressed like I'm auditioning for a part in *Pretty Woman*, you're wrong."

"A little preview couldn't hurt."

I scoffed at the thought. "Do you see anything 'little' about me?"

"Okay, so maybe it would be a 3D preview with

interactive capabilities, but it would work. You know it would."

I sighed as Ava pulled the comb free from the web of hair surrounding it. "Possibly. However, I don't want to win him over with my interactive capabilities. At least, not on the first study date."

"Fine," Ava said, releasing a gush of air as she began spraying down my hair with some sort of syrupy concoction, "win him over with your wit and comedic relief."

"Thanks for the approval."

Ava ignored my snarkiness as she often did and began humming while she worked. Once she applied enough product to my hair that she could get the comb through it, I was allowed to go wash it. After blowing it dry, it continued to be a little disgruntled, but with Ava's honed skillset, she had my bouncy waves in perfect, silky condition within the hour. Just in time for class and, of course, study time with Oliver.

I put on my dress and added my required accessories and fluffed out my hair in the mirror. "It's perfect, Ava. I can't thank you enough."

"My pleasure," she said, gathering up her things. "I expect a full report after your date, though. No more secondhand stories from Sloan."

"Yes. Yes. I promise."

I grabbed my backpack and the rest of my things and followed Ava out. I made sure to leave my phone behind. I didn't want any distractions today. Not that Oliver wasn't the biggest distraction of all. I pushed the thought away and hurried Ava to the elevator. Luckily, I made it to class on time, though my attention to the subject matter was questionable at best.

Non-existent. My attention was non-existent.

I checked my watch after class, even though I knew the time. I had fifteen minutes to make the short commute across campus to the library. Normally, I would speed walk there, in a rush to get to my spot. Today, I took my time. I'd been so worried about my clothes, and my hair, and the never ending voicemails from my father that I'd completely forgotten about what I would I say to him.

What will I say?

People chatted around me on my walk, and I could hear their casual conversations about classes and the latest hit sitcom. The conversation appeared so easy. Natural, almost. It wouldn't be that way for me. I would have to preplan every topic, and practice a couple times in my head. Our previous encounter had been fueled by pure adrenaline. Words practically flowed out my mouth like a fountain on turbo boost. My steps became slower and less purpose driven the closer I got to the giant building with aged brick and hippie inspired architecture. When I made it to the sidewalk at the bottom of the steps, I came to a complete stop.

"I can't do this."

"Yes, you can," said a voice behind me.

I whirled around to find Sloan rushing toward to me with Ava by her side. "What are you doing here?"

"Saving you from yourself," Ava said, grabbing hold of my arm. "I could see the anxiety building in your eyes this morning. I knew you would try to back out."

"And we are here to make sure you don't."

"I can't go in there. I have no idea what I would even say to him."

"Ask him about his crotch," Ava suggested, dragging me up the steps like a dog to the bathtub. "Or his classes. Or his major. Anything."

"It isn't that easy."

"It is, Elle. You did it yesterday. You can do it again."

Scenario after horrible, socially awkward scenario played through my mind. Each one followed by my father's voice, telling me all those things I already knew about myself.

I'm not buying that. Dress like a normal person.

Did you forget how to talk? Well, then, stop sitting there like a knot on a log. People already think you're weird.

"Guys. Sloan. Please. Wait a second." My breath shortened. My heartrate sped up. My knees turned weak and too flexible.

"Sit her down," Sloan instructed, helping me to the step. "Deep breaths, Elle."

I tried to follow her instructions, but the campus in front of me spun. "I just need a minute."

Ava sat beside me. "Forcing you was the wrong answer," she said softly. "So, tell us what we can do to make this easier for you."

Deep breath after deep breath, and finally everything started to come back into focus. "Talk me through it. Step by step. I need to know what to expect."

Sloan rubbed my shoulders. "Okay. You are going to go into the library. Oliver will most likely already be there. You find his table and walk up to him."

I pictured it. This time without all the horrible backlash. "Okay. And then what?"

"And then you be Eloise Duncan," Sloan said matter-of-factly. "You be you in every possible way you can be, because you're amazing."

Tears stung my eyes before I could stop them. Sloan came around in front of me, and she cupped my face in her hands. "I mean that, Elle. You don't need us to tell you what to do, or what to say, because you don't need to be us. Be our sweet, silly, and perfect Eloise."

I hugged her. I hugged them both. I couldn't lose this. Their friendship was everything I ever needed as a kid. Unconditional love that never wavered and always persisted in a way that built me up instead of tearing me down. Breathing suddenly felt a little easier. Screwing things up with Oliver wouldn't be the end of the world. It would suck. But I would still have Sloan and Ava, and in the end, they were what I really needed most in my life. Oliver was a bonus. A wonderful, sexy bonus.

"I don't know what I would do without you two."

After giving myself a few more seconds to get myself together, I stood, allowing that confidence that liked to sneak out at the weirdest times to take control. If Sloan and Ava believed in me, I could at least believe in myself.

"I can do this."

"Damn right," Ava said, hugging me one last time.

I turned to face the door to the library. My fate waited for me, and I knew, deep down inside, that talking to Oliver was one small step toward what would be a lifetime of reclaiming the happiness stripped from me.

It was a necessary step. And I took it without looking back.

Chapter Eight

FULL ENCOUNTER

The library was abnormally loud. Senseless chitchat vibrated my ears as I took the tiniest of steps through the foyer toward Oliver. They were all talking about me. Surely, they were. My awkwardness set off alarms across the campus, signaling a traumatic, embarrassing event was about to take place and everyone should watch and laugh. I rubbed my palms on the black fabric at my hips. Oliver was in his spot. I knew because my brain sent off warning signals.

Abort. Do not proceed.

I took slow, deep breaths, reminding myself of the ease and calmness I'd experienced the previous day talking with Oliver. That could be duplicated. It didn't technically *have* to end in tears and years of therapy sessions. Oliver looked around as soon as I passed the front desk as if he'd been waiting to see me there. His smile was instant. A random and completely weird mix of a giggle and a death wail squeezed past my lips. Thankfully, he was still too far away from me to hear, but the people around me definitely stared now.

To make matters worse, he stood. His hand flexed around the back of the chair as I nervously tucked a piece of my hair behind my ear and gave him an acknowledging wave. "Funny seeing you here," he said before biting the corner of his lip.

"I know, right?" Why was my voicing cracking? "What are the odds?"

He stepped back so I could see the empty chair on the other side, and the clean table in front of it. Normally, his things took over the entire table, probably a ploy to make people not sit there. He'd intentionally not done that today and wanted me to notice. My hands clasped the strap of my backpack to hold me in place. "Thanks again for the offer."

"Of course." He motioned me to the seat, and I took it. "I finished all my homework this morning, so you have my full attention."

Again, a quiet, yet horribly embarrassing noise escaped my mouth. It was the sound of my stomach hitting my heels.

His full attention. I would have his *full* attention.

"You didn't have to do that because of me."

"I offered to help. I want to help." He pulled out a couple of books from his backpack on the floor. "And look. I found some really cool study aids for your class at the bookstore."

I scratched my head, taking in his bright, vibrant smile and the books in his hands. "I'm sorry. Did you just say really cool and study aids in the same sentence?"

Oliver laughed. "Yes. And if you hang around me enough, you will unfortunately hear me use much worse blasphemy."

Oh. Now I was intrigued. "Like what?"

He leaned in closer. "Like exciting experiment and chemistry fun."

My cheesy grin was undeniable. "Do they sell bottles of whatever you're taking that makes you think that stuff? Because I really need it."

Oliver smiled and set the books on the table. "C'mon. You have to enjoy school a little bit, right? Why else go to college?"

I bit the inside of my jaw. That was the thing. I currently majored in business, despite my father's wishes, only because I thought it would come in handy when I opened my own bakery. If it were up to me, which nothing in my life seemed to be, I probably would have skipped college altogether. Baking was my dream. I should have gone to culinary school.

The thought stung my brain. I hadn't even mentioned the idea to my father. I tried bringing up the subject of alternatives to college once, and I spent three weekends at home confined to my room because, apparently, my "friends" were putting crazy ideas in my head.

"Yeah," I said simply, because I had no other choice but to agree.

I took one of the books on the table and flipped through it. "Thanks for the aids. How much were they? I'll pay you back."

Oliver placed his hand on the book. "No. I wanted to buy them. Besides, anatomy is a general ed course. I'll have to take it soon too. I'll reuse them."

I was taken aback by his kindness, but then I remembered the poster in my backpack. I grabbed the brown tube I stored it in and handed it to him. "What if I trade you?"

His fingers inched closer to mine. He almost touched them. He almost touched me. "Is that the X-Men poster for Dex?"

"Yes. It's sealed up tight. You can ship it to him just like this."

Oliver grinned, turning the tube over in his hands as if he could see the poster inside. "He is going to freak out. I can't thank you enough."

"Call us even."

His lips were so close. And then suddenly they weren't. He turned back around, placing the poster in his bag, then he opened one of the other books. "I took the liberty of filling out the first section of this study form you need based on the terms you practiced yesterday."

I caught my breath. I hadn't even realized I'd lost it. I nodded vigorously as I focused on the task at hand. This was a study session. Not an actual date. I settled into my seat, washing the vision of his lips out of my mind. The more I listened to Oliver explain the study aid he'd bought, the more my nerves seemed to settle down. He was actually a good tutor. He was detailed and always paused for questions and clarified when I needed it. If it weren't for his devastating good looks and fantasy driven voice, it could have been a really smart idea to study with Oliver.

However, Oliver Edwards was devastatingly handsome. And his voice, the one where I honed in on the deep octaves instead of the actual words, made me imagine anatomy in a way that would not help me pass my class. I was so doomed. Hellaciously turned on, but definitely doomed.

"Okay," he said finally, after a twenty-minute lecture I didn't hear. "I want you to go through the guide yourself, and when you think you're ready. I'll test you."

There was my stomach again, playing footsy with my toes. I cleared my throat of my shame. "Test me?"

"Yes." Smile. Why did things such as a test make him smile like that? "Tests are very informative of your progress."

I nodded. "Informative. Yes. That they are."

I didn't need another test to tell me I would fail.

Oliver's fingers grazed my elbow and then…his thumb caressed its way across the hem of my sleeve. "Don't stress. I have a proven method to help you focus."

He had a proven method, all right, but it wasn't to help me focus. I involuntarily crossed my legs under the table and clenched my teeth. No sounds were coming out of my mouth. Not a single one. My eyebrows rose in order to inquire about his methods of continuous torture. He eagerly pulled out his phone and a set of earphones. "Music." He handed the ears buds to me. "I have a study play list I listen to at home sometimes. It helps block out the world around me."

I didn't want to block out those blue eyes. Hell,

if that was all it took, I could study at home. I wanted to see him…hear him…seduce him among the adventures I used to only dream about. Oliver handed me the earphones, and I put them in because he wanted me to. He started the first song, and it wasn't anything I expected. I'm not sure what I expected—maybe a symphony orchestra? Bach or Mozart? Instead, I heard nothing but water. Waves, to be exact. Angry waves crashing against a shore. I could see them so perfectly. The white mist rising into the air, fighting back against the hard stone that blocked its path inland.

My shoulders instantly relaxed. Oliver, apparently pleased his tactic was already working, moved the book in front of me and pulled out another for himself. He started reading without saying anything else, and I took that as my cue to get to work. I wasn't entirely focused on the book or my test, but I also wasn't totally absentminded. I could feel Oliver's presence next to me as I read. I no longer had to glance up every minute to make sure he was still there. I knew he was there, and it was comforting.

An hour and a half later, I pulled the ear phones out and handed Oliver back his phone. "I'm ready," I said confidently, and I was indeed confident. Sitting there with Oliver was the most studying I'd done in months. Maybe this arrangement really could work out? You know, as long as the boy didn't do anything crazy like kiss me. There would be no hope if he kissed me.

Oliver put his book away and pulled the study guide to him. "Okay. Let me find the diagram and go make a copy of it."

My hand moved over into the seat as Oliver vacated it as if I was a magnet drawn to his sexy opposing force. I blew out a breath when he left and tried to regain my composure. This entire day was one giant mental drain. I straightened the bottom of my dress, patiently waiting for him to return. A girl two tables away stared at him as he passed by her, and it caught my attention. Jealousy seeped from every pore on her body. I almost laughed, but in my lifetime I'd gotten a lot of looks from people, but jealousy? That was new. It had everything to do with Oliver, but still new. I also liked it a lot more than I should have. A morally sound person would have felt sad at the thought of my glorious luck bringing someone else pain. I did not feel sad for the girl. In fact, it took effort for me to not stick my tongue out at her and laugh.

Oliver returned with my test, and with the girl's unwavering glare still on me, I scooted my seat a fraction of an inch closer to him, claiming my territory. The girl got up and left.

Good idea on her part.

I took my test, and to my surprise, I did pretty well. Oliver turned the paper around and displayed it to me proudly. "See. Now you know what you need to work on before your class tomorrow."

"Thanks," I said, scanning the few terms I'd gotten mixed up. I'd never felt so confident about an upcoming quiz, and the relief allowed me to breathe in a way that was unconfined.

Oliver's fingers grazed my shoulder before permanently planting themselves there. He squeezed it gently. "You're going to do great tomorrow."

My cheeks flushed, and heat prickled the back of my neck. I wasn't accustomed to this kind of encouragement.

You are going to do great tomorrow as opposed to *you better do great tomorrow*.

I involuntarily glanced toward my backpack. Why couldn't I stop worrying about my father's approval? I wanted out from his under his thumb, and I'd always planned that going away to college would be my way out, but it didn't feel that way now. The farther I ran, the more restricted I felt. As if his rules followed me here, a noose around my willpower that slowly tightened and tightened, until I finally wavered from my own dreams.

He would hate Oliver and everything about him. Bartholomew would demand I end contact with him the same way he demanded I cancel my prom date.

"Elle?"

I glanced up. Oliver's hand remained on my shoulder. "Are you okay?"

"Yeah." I wasn't. I'd never been, but the lie almost felt like the truth.

The warmth of his hand fell from my shoulder as he glanced at his watch. "I need to get to class, but…"

I held my breath, waiting for him to continue. His gaze darted around as if not sure where to go.

"But…" I encouraged, my hands folding anxiously in my lap.

His smile was shy. "I'll be here next week. In this spot like I always am."

89

I swallowed, testing my voice first. "I'll be here next week too. Like I always am."

He fiddled awkwardly with the corner of one of his books. "Maybe I'll see you."

Why did he look so rattled all of a sudden? "I'm sure you will."

He nodded affirmatively as if we'd made another study date, though technically we hadn't. He started gathering up his things, and I did the same. I bent over to pick up my backpack, and when I stood, I found Oliver's eye on me. All of me.

He instantly glanced away, but it was too late. He'd been caught. He bit his lip as he threw his backpack around his shoulders. "Those tights. I've never seen anything like that."

I smiled sweetly at him. He hadn't been looking at my tights. I wouldn't embarrass him further, though, so I played along. My tights, black like my dress, were lace and made a rose pattern all the way down my legs to my boots. "I like to be different."

"Nothing wrong with that."

We stood behind our chairs, the time ticking down on the giant clock on the wall. He compared the time on it to his watch and sighed. "I really do have to go."

"Me too," I assured him. "I'll see you next week."

We parted ways, as in I went the opposite direction toward the bathroom, even though I didn't technically need to go. I only wanted to make the departure less weird and drawn out. Once inside the safety of the first stall, I finally exhaled. I leaned back against the door and closed my eyes. Before I knew it, my hand covered my mouth to keep the excessive giggles from bursting out of it.

Oliver Edwards liked me.

At least…I thought so.

He demonstrated all the signs that would indicate a boy liked you. He definitely checked me out. I hadn't realized how fast my heart beat until it finally started to slow down. Exhilarated couldn't even come close to describing the euphoria that erupted inside of me.

Chapter Nine

THE QUIZ

The cafeteria was crowded. I sat quietly, snugged between Sloan and the wall of our booth, reviewing my list of terms one last time before class. Ava fiddled with her plate of pasta while glancing around the room, still pouting that Brad never came here.

"So, what's the plan?" Sloan asked, turning in her seat to face me. "Are you two going to study together again?"

"Maybe." I kept my eyes focused on the terms, trying to engrain the list into my head. "We sort of left it open."

Ava put her fork down. "What do you mean?"

I rubbed my eyes; a deep-rooted thud pounded behind them. "I mean we said we would see each other next week. We didn't set an exact day or time."

Sloan eased closer. "But you will go talk to him again, right? If you see him there. No more pining away from across the room."

I rolled my eyes. "You're one to talk."

"I'm serious, Eloise. It went well yesterday. You won't try to talk yourself out of it again, will you?"

They knew me too well. I always tried to talk myself out everything that was good for me. Yet, the bad things. I had so much trouble letting them go. "Yes. I will talk to him."

"Good." Finally, Sloan seemed satisfied and went back to her burger. She bit off a giant mouthful then stared at me before swallowing. "Aren't you going to eat dinner?"

I fiddled with the corner of the paper, folding and unfolding it. "I'm too nervous to eat."

Sloan frowned at me. "Don't let him do this to you."

I looked away. "Sloan—"

"I'm serious. I hate seeing you like this, and for what reason? Because you're scared to tell your dad you're failing a class? Screw him."

"He pays my tuition."

"You can get loans like the rest of us. No, it's not ideal, but it's also not worth keeping him in your life. The money is an excuse, and you know it."

I knew it. Of course I did. It didn't change the fact that I still hadn't told my father off. That I still hadn't told him about my grades...about my dreams. Ava reached across the table and nudged Sloan's elbow. "It's not the time. She's already upset. You'll only make it worse."

Sloan scooted into my side and hugged me. "I'm trying to make it better. You have a family. You don't need him. We love you. We love you the way you're supposed to love somebody."

I hid my face in her hair so they couldn't see the tears. I hugged her back. I knew all those things too. And I was so thankful for them. "Eat," I said, going back to my paper. "I'll grab something on my way from class once I pass this quiz."

"Promise?"

"Yes. I just need to make sure I get these last ten terms correct before six o'clock."

"Umm…Elle. It's fifteen till six. Maybe you should go ahead and leave for class."

"What?" I scrambled to grab my phone and check the time. Sloan was right. I only had fifteen minutes until my test started. "Crap."

I threw everything into my bag as Sloan moved out of the way to let me out of the booth. "Call us with the results," Ava yelled as I took off.

I gave them a wave and weaved my way through the crowd. I squeezed through a group of students and out the door, hopping down the long row of steps to the sidewalk. The chilly spring air bit at my face, but I didn't take the time to pull up the hood of my coat. It wouldn't help the sting on my legs anyway. I rounded the corner of the building, expecting to see the science building in the distance. Instead, there was an eclipse. It happened instantly. The building I'd seen a thousand times disappeared before my eyes, replaced by something so close to my face that it blurred together, turning everything black…until I slammed into it.

The impact was hard. A stone wall covered in flannel. I grabbed at the familiar fabric to catch my balance, but it was too late. I catapulted backward, landing on the hard concrete. The tights on my left thigh ripped against impact and so did the skin on my left hand. I clutched it against my chest, the blood sprinkling to the surface.

"Elle. Are you okay?"

Oliver. Of course it was him. Wasn't he destined to witness every humiliating feat I'd ever accomplished? I warily glanced up. In the dim light of the evening, I barely recognized him. He wore the familiar red flannel shirt I liked, but he had on a jet black jacket with the hood pulled up. His shaggy brown hair was barely visible, cascading down around his glasses.

"Yes." I clutched my hand tighter to my chest. I didn't want him to see it. "I was in a hurry. I'm sorry."

Oliver didn't see my hand, not because of my stealth like concealment, but because his gaze was on my legs. The rip in the tights led up underneath my dress that just so happened to be jerked up high on my thigh. I reflexively pulled the hem down, and Oliver came out of his daze and held his hand out for me. I took it with my right hand and let him help me up. His smile was soft as he held me steady. "You know…there are better ways to say hello."

My cheeks lit up like fireworks. "Again. Sorry."

He was so close. So fatally close. His breath brushed across my hair. "Don't be. Please. I was actually just thinking about you. Are you on your way to your class?"

"Yes. And I'm running behind." I pulled my phone out of my pocket. "I only have five minutes."

Oliver nodded. "I won't keep you."

Yet…he didn't move. He blocked my way. I could still see nothing but his perfect silhouette. He swallowed, his gaze dropping from my eyes to my lips then back again. "Would you like to study together again next week? I realized after the fact that we didn't exactly set a time next week."

"Sure. When are you free?"

I would be free anytime for him.

"I have a chemistry experiment due Tuesday morning. I have to spend most of the day Monday in the lab. Tuesday afternoon?"

I nodded quickly. "Okay. I finish for the day around three."

"I'll be there."

"Great. I'll bring my study guides."

He grinned and stepped out of my path. The view of the science building returned. "Good luck. I know you'll do great."

I stuck my hurt hand in my pocket and picked up my backpack with the other. "Thanks. I'll see you Tuesday."

His smile grew wider. "Tuesday."

I walked toward the building, but I could feel his gaze on me. When I made it to the steps, I stopped and turned around. Oliver still stood on the corner, watching me. He waved, and my heart…something inside of it I thought had died long ago started ticking again.

I held it as I rushed up the steps to my class. Maybe Sloan was right. I wasn't alone in the world anymore. There were other people now…people like her and Ava who were my family. They cared about me the way family was supposed to care about each other. I thought of Oliver as I sat at my desk. I had him now too. Nothing was permanent, but there were other people in the world who liked me.

Me.

Just the way I was.

And that meant something. Something so much more important than this grade on my quiz. The nerves that plagued me in the cafeteria vanished. Failing anatomy wouldn't be the end of the world. Maybe the end of my relationship with the only parent I had left, but maybe that was a good thing.

No. It would be a good thing.

I could pass anatomy. I could let my father's influence on me go. I could talk to the boy of my dreams.

I could do it all. Anything I wanted to do.

I pressed my pencil to the paper in front of me, reading the first question. All I had to do now was prove it to myself.

Chapter Ten

CHEMISTRY LAB

I made a B on my quiz. I was pretty ecstatic about it, despite the fact that it wouldn't help me bring my grade up enough to please my father. Not that an A would please him. Nothing I did was ever good enough. I was my mother's daughter. Nothing I could do would be good enough for Bartholomew Duncan, because every time he looked at me, he still saw her. The woman he couldn't control. I was simply too much like her to be loved.

Ava bumped into me, knocking me out of reverie. I'd been staring at my reflection in the window of the Student Services building. I could almost see my mother in myself, especially on days like today. The damp weather caused my waves to loosen, and the wind blew them haphazardly around my face. It reminded me so much of her. At least, what little of her I still held in my memory. It'd been so long since I'd seen her face, sometimes I feared I'd forgotten, and I was simply making up the details.

That long blue sweater she always wore in the mornings that had a hole in the sleeve, stitched up with yellow thread. Was that real?

"Hello," Ava said, shaking my arm. "Earth to Eloise."

I blinked and turned around. "Sorry, I've been lost in my own thoughts all morning."

"Still celebrating your awesome quiz grade?"

I faked a smile. "Something like that. What did you say you wanted to do before lunch?"

Ava straightened her backpack. "I need to go by my biology class and pick up my homework. My professor is allowing us to use the study questions as prep for our test."

The word biology instantly perked me up. "What building is that in?"

"Carver. Why?"

A wicked smile snaked across my face. It was Monday. Oliver said he would be in the chemistry lab all day on Monday. "All of the science classes are in Carver, right?"

"I think so." Ava eyed me suspiciously. "What are you planning?"

I shrugged. "Nothing. Simply hoping I might catch a glimpse of Oliver in his natural environment."

Ava smirked as we started walking. "Can't make it until tomorrow for your fix?"

"I'm not going to hunt him down. But if we happen to walk by his lab, it couldn't hurt to peek inside."

Ava shook her head mockingly. "You've got it

bad, Elle."

I followed Ava to the Carver building and upstairs to her professor's office. The secretary said he was in his classroom preparing for his next lecture. We went back downstairs, and I peeked inside every classroom along the way, but saw nothing that looked like a chemistry lab. I waited outside the room as Ava went to see her professor. I stepped down the hallway to a set of windows. No other classrooms on this floor had windows. Sure enough, inside the room was a lab. Tables sectioned off with burners and beakers filled with odd colored liquids. Several students huddled around tables, some taking notes while others stirred bowls and measured out formulas.

It was definitely the chemistry lab. But there was no Oliver to be found.

I slumped against the window, disappointed.

"Elle?"

My hand clamped against the glass like a suction cup. I was wrong. Oliver was here. I just didn't realize how close. I glanced over my shoulder, and I was sure I winced at the sight of him. I'd been caught red handed. "Hey, Oliver."

The boy had on a lab coat with protective goggles pushed up on his forehead, sending his hair in erratic directions. If they ever made a mad sexy scientist calendar, Oliver could be the cover. His smile was sweet, but surprised. "What are you doing in the science building?"

I finally managed to turn my body completely around. I tried to say something. My lips moved to articulate the words, but my voice refused to participate. Ava came out of the room down the hall and I pointed at her. Oliver, waiting patiently for me get myself under control, followed my finger. "Ava," I finally managed to get out. "I came with her. She had to pick up notes."

"Oh. So, does that mean you're not in a hurry?"

My brows twisted together, and he must have caught on to my confusion. He grabbed my hand. "I would love to show you around the lab, if you have time. Your friend can come along as well. I've been studying all day. I could really use a break."

My lips parted, my gaze dropping to my hand that he still held. Ava spotted us and laughed. I probably looked like one of those mimes you met on the street. Was I trying to get out of a box, or not hug him into a million nerdy little pieces?

"I think we have time for that."

Ava's gaze never left our connected hands as she approached. Her smile almost reached her ears. "Time for what?"

Oliver moved next to me, his hand still clasped gently around mine. "I'm offering a tour of my lab. Interested?"

My best friend instantly turned into a supervillain. She might as well have grown a mustache and twirled the ends as she stood over my bound body on the train tracks. "You know what, I would have really loved that, but my professor just asked me if I would drop this paper off to Professor Curry across campus. I bet Elle would love to, though."

Liar. Liar. Push-up bra on fire.

How could I be angry at her, though? She was

gifting me alone time with Oliver in his lab. I officially owed her something. Something really awesome.

"Maybe next time." Oliver adjusted his goggles, not really appearing too disappointed by Ava's reply. "You ready?"

I glanced between him and Ava. Was I ready?

Ava didn't think so, because she practically bubbled at the seams with laughter at my frantic, freaking out state. I straightened my shoulders and nodded. Ava gave me an encouraging nudge on the shoulder. "Talk to you later," she sang, smirking triumphantly.

I squeaked as Oliver tugged on my hand. He led me further down the hallway to the door. When he let go of my hand and turned around, I finally found my sanity again. At least, what little sanity I had left. "Are you sure I'm not interrupting your study day?"

"Of course not. I've already successfully completed the formula three times today. I've mostly been goofing around for the last hour."

"Goofing around?"

He opened the door and held it for me. "I know...those words and chemistry don't go together, right?"

I smiled coyly. "I reserve judgment. You think you can change my mind?"

His gaze raked down my body from my head to the tip of my Emerald City green shoes. "I'm willing to give it my best shot."

He walked off toward one of the stations in the back of the room, and it was a good thing. I was about to rip that lab coat off him.

We bypassed the other students in the classroom. None of them even glanced up as we swerved by their station. Oliver pulled an extra stool up to the long black counter then moved his backpack to the floor. "So, first things first. How did you do on your quiz?"

I looked down, my fingers intertwining with the edge of my jacket. "I made an eighty-eight."

He ducked down to catch my gaze. "I really want to say awesome job, but you look disappointed with that."

"No. I'm not disappointed."

His brow creased. "Am I missing something?"

I would not tell Oliver about my father. I couldn't.

"I would really like to bring my grade up as high as I can possibly manage by the end of the semester. An A on my weekly quizzes would go a long way toward that goal."

Oliver pursed his lips. "Okay. We can work on that, then. The goal for next week is a perfect score."

He looked utterly excited by the challenge. His eyes lit up in this beautiful, bright way, like they were on fire. That boy had a love affair with studying, and I was completely jealous. I scooted suggestively toward him. "Enough about me. When do I get this tour?"

He leaned on the counter, his fingers reaching out to tip the empty beaker in front of him. "Give me five minutes."

I cocked my head to the side. "Why five

minutes?"

He nodded toward the group of students in front of us that busily rushed back and forth around their station. "They always leave at noon for lunch." He glanced up at me, his smile something more than sweet. "Always."

I sucked in a breath. If they left, that would mean Oliver and I would be alone. In his laboratory. With that lab coat on and those goggles.

Damn those goggles. They were worse than his glasses.

I settled onto my stool, but Oliver didn't sit. He remained leaned on the counter, closer to me. "So, how was your weekend?"

I shrugged. "Long. Exhausting."

He appeared surprised. "Really?"

"I worked all weekend," I explained.

His hand slid over in front of me on the counter. His eyes danced. "Where do you work?"

I grabbed the edge of the stool, cursing myself. Why did I bring up work? That was the absolute last thing I should have brought up. I couldn't tell him I worked at the bakery. I couldn't tell him I was the cupcake girl. The humiliation would be too much. I relaxed my shoulders, attempting to appear bored and unrattled by his question. "The same place every other college kid works. I serve food to people."

"I thought I'd been to every restaurant in town. I haven't seen you."

My heart thudded at a race horse pace in my chest. I had to get the topic off me and back on him. "Every restaurant in town? Don't you ever eat at

104

home?"

He laughed. "I'm not exactly a good cook."

I breathed a sigh of relief when the other students started packing up their things. It caught Oliver's attention and he forgot about his interrogation. I hated that I thought of it like that. Oliver simply wanted to get to know me better, and because of my crazy actions, I turned it into something weird. There was nothing I could do about it now. I'd given him the cupcakes.

When the last student left the room, Oliver pushed back from the counter. "Do you like gummy bears?"

"Umm...sure. Gummy bears are good." They weren't cupcakes, but they were sugar, so they were mostly acceptable.

"Would you be offended if I violently destroyed one?"

"Why would you squish a gummy bear?"

Mad Scientist. Oliver was definitely a Mad Scientist. "I'm going to do something much worse than squish it." He grabbed my hand and led me to the front of the room. "Can you get me one of the big test tubes?"

"Sure."

Oliver crossed the room and unlocked a black cabinet in the corner. I brought him the test tube, and he poured a white liquid into it. "What's that?"

"Molten potassium chlorate. My task for the experiment tomorrow is to demonstrate a reaction. Some of the other students are doing simple things like Diet Coke and Mentos. And, sure, it's cool. It will erupt like a volcano."

I watched him carefully as he closed the cabinet and went back to his station. "And what will potassium chlorate do to a gummy bear?"

He appeared exceptionally pleased that I asked. "Oh, just wait and see."

He screwed the test tube into a metal holder and then retrieved a bag of red gummy bears from his backpack. He took one out and handed it to me. "Hold this a moment."

I cupped the bear in my hand while Oliver took a small flame from the burner and heated up the liquid in the bottom of the tube. Then he pulled his goggles down over his glasses and reached for the bear. He started to put it into the tube, but then paused, looking over his shoulder at me. "You should probably step back a little more."

I laughed. "It can't be that bad."

Oliver physically moved me back three more feet. "Trust me on this one."

I stayed safely where he put me, and it was a good thing. Oliver pushed the gummy bear into the test tube and quickly jerked his hand away. As soon as it hit the white liquid, a giant spark erupted from the tube. And another. Red and pink fireworks sprang from the inside as the gummy bear cracked and popped like a kernel in a bag of popcorn. I scooted back a little more.

"Holy crap. How did you know it would do that?"

Oliver shrugged like it was no big deal. "I did a little research."

"Of course you did."

The poor test tube continued to flame up, sparks

flying out of the end. I worried it might take off like a rocket. It probably would have if Oliver hadn't screwed it into the metal frame. "So, do you think that will get me an A over all those volcanic Mentos?"

"Definitely."

The reaction finally burned out, leaving nothing but bits and pieces of what appeared to be white foam in the test tube. He carefully touched the glass to check if it was still hot. "I'm really glad I ran into you today."

"Yeah?"

He didn't look at me, but I could still see his small smile as he unscrewed the tube from the frame. "Yeah. I've been looking forward to our study session tomorrow."

"You really do love to study more than anyone I know."

He took the tube over to the sink and turned on the water. He glanced over his shoulder at me, pulling his goggles up so I could see the seriousness in his eyes. "I think you've misjudged my intentions."

No, I hadn't. I only wanted him to call me out on it. Oliver Edwards's intentions were crystal clear in the way he looked at me. He studied me like one of his books. His speculative gaze lit my skin on fire.

The door opened behind me. It was the only thing saving my libido from taking my common sense hostage. More students were back from their lunch. "Hey, Oliver," one of the boys in the back yelled. "Would you help us with our Briggs-Rancher Reaction?"

Oliver's lips went into a straight line as he turned the water off. "It's Briggs-Rauscher."

"Yeah. Yeah." The boy ran a clueless hand through his hair. "Can you help us?"

Oliver placed his goggles on the counter. "I'm busy right now, Brett."

The boy, Brett, who I instantly didn't like, looked at me and chuckled. "Is this your idea of a date, Edwards?"

Yes.

I moved toward him, my hand gripped around a piece of lab equipment I seriously considered chucking at the idiot's head. Oliver's hand wound into the back of my jacket, tugging me back. His arm went around my waist. "There's this thing called Google, Brett. You should try it. Though, to warn you, it still requires you to read. So, good luck with that."

Oliver grabbed his backpack and motioned me forward. I begrudgingly followed his lead, but I still shot Brett a dirty look. *I'm crazy*, the look implied. *Don't mess with my nerd.*

Once outside the classroom, Oliver breathed again. "I'm sorry about that. Unfortunately, Brett's manners are as deficient as his brain cells."

"You don't actually help that asshole with his homework, do you?"

Oliver laughed. "Hell, no. It's not my responsibility to teach a caveman to make fire. Besides, he only asked because you were there."

"What do you mean?"

Again, Oliver looked at me. My lips. My crescent moon earrings. My neck where my heart

108

beat. "Would you like to go get lunch?"

"I'd love to." I glanced at my watch and slumped when I read the time. "But I have class."

"Tomorrow, then," he said instantly. "The library like we planned."

I nodded. "I'll be there."

I'd be there with bells and butterflies, come hell, high water, or an apocalyptic event. Even then, I would kill zombies to get to Oliver.

"Could I walk you to class?"

Nod. Nod. Nod. I had bobbleheaditis again.

Oliver nudged my elbow with his, and we started off toward my class. I would have to unintentionally run into him more often.

Chapter Eleven

STUDY BUDDY

Tuesday came, and so did Wednesday and Thursday. Oliver and I started a new routine. We were officially study partners. We met at the library almost every day. Every glorious, perfect day. We moved to a larger table on the other side of the main floor lobby so we would both have enough room for our large array of books. It was *our* table.

I'd managed a halfway decent grade on my quiz last week, but if I wanted to survive my father's wrath, I had to do better. A lot better. Yes, despite my pep talk, I still worried about it. Bartholomew Duncan wasn't the kind of dad to let you start being in control. I didn't tell Oliver about the stakes, and everything I had to lose, but he knew I really needed to bring my grade up. He didn't ask why, so I didn't offer an explanation. He was perfect like that. In those rare moments we weren't enjoying the peace and quiet together, we talked about everything.

We talked about our favorite books, comics and classics, and our favorite music, which boiled down to anything we could torture doing karaoke alone in our cars. He told me about his dream to be a chemical engineer, and I told him about my dream to own a business. I didn't mention the cupcakes.

I couldn't.

Oliver still didn't know those cupcakes that mysteriously showed up on his book every day belonged to me. I would either show up early for our study session and sneak him a cupcake before I officially arrived, or wait until I left and then circle back around and leave one.

Yes. I was crazy.

I was well aware of the exact amount of crazy it took to pull off such a scam, but I couldn't bear to tell Oliver the truth. I loved the way he smiled at me. I loved his stories and his vast array of ridiculous t-shirts. I didn't want to jeopardize this good thing we had going by admitting I'd been, and still was, secretly admiring him.

I had a box of cupcakes in my backpack, awaiting deployment. It would have to wait until after our study session, though. I had another quiz tomorrow. In perfect nerd fashion, Oliver was bound and determined to make sure I got an A this time. He made a copy of my list of terms for the week, and handed me back the original.

He took the top half and I took the bottom as we began writing everything out. About halfway through, I noticed him glancing around, and then I heard a distinct rumbling sound coming from the direction of his stomach. I nudged his elbow. "You okay there, champ?"

He leaned back in the seat and rubbed his stomach. "Yeah, I missed breakfast this morning. I was kind of counting on..." He threw another glance around the room, but then stopped.

I sat up a little straighter. "You were counting on what?"

He grinned and turned his head away from me.

I leaned over to see his face. "Are you blushing?"

I couldn't resist. Oliver blushing was just about the sexiest thing I had ever seen. I could think of about a hundred different ways to make that boy blush, and eleven different positions.

"It's nothing, really. Trust me, you don't want to know."

"Oh, but I do." I inched closer. "Oh, I really, really do."

He fiddled with his hands in his lap as he blew out a breath. He was going to be difficult. Always playing hard to get. Oliver didn't know, but I was determined to be reigning champ at Capture the Nerd. I placed my hand on the back of his chair and leaned my body toward his. "Tell me."

"Someone usually leaves me a cupcake. At least, they have been for the past couple weeks," he blurted out, his cheeks beaming a glossy red.

Everything inside of me knotted up. "Oh, really? Who?"

He shrugged. "I have no idea. I get up to go to the bathroom, or to get a book. When I come back, it's sitting there."

I examined his face, and his stomach let out

112

another rumble. I smiled sweetly at him. "Are you wanting your cupcake?"

A slight smile crept across his face. "They're really good." Then his smile turned down at the edges. "I don't know why they don't give it to me when I'm sitting here."

I made my eyes stay on Oliver and not look down at my backpack containing the box of cupcakes that seemed to be calling my name. "Umm, well, you could always go and see what happens," I suggested. "I'd really hate for you to miss out on your cupcake because of me."

He pushed his glasses back up his nose. "Are you being serious?"

I rolled my eyes. "Go, cupcake freak." I laughed, pushing him out of his seat. "Go get a book or take a walk down the street. I promise if some stranger drops a cupcake off, I won't touch it."

He eyed me warily as he stood, and I motioned him on. "Go."

As soon as he turned the corner, I jerked my cell out of my bag, hitting the first button on my speed dial.

"Sloan?" I was in panic mode. "Where are you?"

Sloan's voice sang angelically back to me. "Today is officially ride a cowboy day." I could practically see her bouncing as she skipped down the street. "I'm on my way to the café to see Preston. Want to come watch me make a fool of myself?"

"No. I need you to come to the library right now."

"Why?" Her voice dropped down to a whisper.

"You didn't kidnap him, did you? Because I'm pretty sure you should ask his permission before you gag someone."

"Sloan." I did not have time for her jokes right now. "I need you to listen to me. I think he has a thing for the cupcake girl. He left to see if she would leave him a cupcake, but I can't leave him a cupcake because then he would ask me about the girl, and the girl would be me! So, I need you to come here right now and get the cupcake and put it on his book while I distract him."

There was long pause. "Oh my gosh, Elle...you should have just gagged him."

I kept glancing back over my shoulder for signs of Oliver. "Sloan, please. I need my best friend. Help me."

Sloan sighed. "Okay, okay, I'm on my way."

I clicked my phone off and glanced impatiently over my shoulder trying to calculate how long it would take her to get here. Within a couple of minutes, I spotted Oliver walking back down the corridor in my direction. A very distinctive disappointed pout came across his lips as his eyes raked the desk in front of me. "No luck, sweet tooth," I explained, using my best Vanna White impression to showcase the empty desk. "She's obviously not going to show herself in my presence."

He looked at me, still frustrated. "You think I made her up, don't you?"

I couldn't stop the grin. Oh, I knew she was real. A little light on the sanity and a little heavy on the nerd appreciation, but real nonetheless.

114

"She is real," he said.

I raised a questioning brow. "She? How do you know for sure it's a she?"

A look of pure disappointment engulfed him, and I burst out laughing. So darn cute. He definitely hadn't considered that option. Out of the corner of my eye, I saw Sloan pretending to read a book next to the magazine rack. I jumped out of my seat. "How about we both leave and see what happens?"

"Okay." He looked at me, his lips pressed tighter together. "She is real, though."

I glanced over my shoulder and pointed to the black bag on the floor and quickly followed after him. "So how long should we give this imagin— mystery person of yours?"

His brows knotted. "You are going to feel really bad when we come back and there is a cupcake sitting on that desk."

No. I was going to feel really tortured watching him eat it. "If there is a cupcake sitting on that desk, I will personally cook you a five course meal."

Because tricking your dream guy into a date is almost as good as dislocating his balls. "There will be a cupcake on that desk," he said, as if convincing himself.

We waited a few minutes as he impatiently browsed the books along the shelf at the other end of the library. He busied himself reading the previews, and I busied myself with figuring out how long it would take to get his pants off. He placed the book back on the shelf and looked over at me. I knew that was his cue for he'd waited long enough. I motioned him forward. "Lead the way."

We walked silently back out toward his desk, and sure enough, two of my pink cupcakes sat on his book. Damn Sloan. She was only supposed to put one. I never left more than one. I didn't want to risk him offering it to someone else. His pace quickened as he saw it, and I swore I saw him hop once. "I told you." He beamed, picking up the cupcakes.

"Yeah, yeah, so you win." I tried to appear as if I wasn't happy. "I guess I owe you a meal."

As the words left my mouth, my breath caught. Sitting beneath the cupcakes he had picked up was a little pink note. My heart sank.

Damn freaking Sloan.

He picked it up and unfolded it. It took everything in me not to grab it out of his hands. His eyes ran down the note and his cheeks suddenly flashed red.

I leaned up on my tiptoes. "W-w-what does it say?"

Because God only knew what Sloan would come up with. I wouldn't surprise me if she used explicit diagrams. His cheeks flashed red again and he bit his lip.

"Oliver?"

His gaze dropped to the floor and he crumbled the note in a fist. He turned his face away from me and pushed his glasses back up his nose. "Um." His lips pressed tight together and he unconsciously adjusted his glasses. "I think...I think maybe they are making fun of me?"

My heart sank. "What do you mean?"

He let out a small sigh and turned further away

from me. "I think maybe it's someone having fun at my expense."

At his expense? Oh, hell no. "What does the note say?"

He shook his head. "It's okay, Elle. I'm used to being the nerd. It's nothing new."

"The note," I said, and this time it wasn't a request. "Give me the note."

Embarrassment flooded him and his fingers unwound one by one, revealing the crumbled pink paper. I quickly grabbed it and smoothed out the edges.

In pretty swirling letters I read:

Made with obsession for the nerd of my dreams.

I raised my eyes back to his, but he wouldn't look at me. He ran his fingers through his hair and sighed. "I feel really stupid," he mumbled, staring at the floor. "I should have known better."

I opened my mouth, but words didn't come out. I wanted to tell him that he took it all wrong. The note wasn't making fun of him. It was the truth. Sloan had written no lies, but how could I tell him that? His emotions were vaguely flashing through his eyes, and I stood motionless before him.

Hurt. Embarrassment. Pain.

I crumbled the note in my hand and threw it on the table.

Sloan was dead.

However, Oliver Edwards was not about to leave this library thinking he was anything other than the hottest freaking thing to ever grace the corrupted inner workings of my mind. I stepped forward and grabbed his shirt, pulling him until he was inches from my face with a little more force than he was ready for.

He stumbled forward into me. He looked down, staring at the hand gripped around his shirt, and I heard him swallow before he looked me back in the eye. "Elle?"

I jerked him again and his mouth clamped shut. I was going to do the talking and he was going to listen. I intensified my grip on him and scooted up until I knew my breath would hit his face. He needed to hear this, and I needed to say it. No more sidelines for Eloise. It was time I got in the game.

"Listen to me, Oliver. I need to explain something to you, and I'm only going to say it once." I took a gulp of air, pulling myself up to look him dead in the eye. "You're a nerd, and you're hot. Get used to it."

Chapter Twelve

SURPRISE

I'd obviously lost my mind. Tee totally, rattling around, nothing but rocks, lost it. Here I was with my hand gripped around Oliver's shirt like I was ready for an eight second ride in the middle of the library. Not only that, but my dumb ass told him he was a hot nerd. I said it to his face. *Out loud.*

There was no backing down now. It was time to suck it up and tell the truth. Oliver's lips parted. He gaped at me like I'd spoken death threats to him in Chinese. I slowly loosened my grip on his shirt. I wanted him to get my point, not scare him out of his skinny jeans. "That note was not making fun of you."

Those beautiful blues eyes beamed down at me. "But," he began, and I shook my head with a silencing click of my tongue.

"Nerds are hot, Oliver," I said again. "Rainbow orgasmically hot. That is a fact you are going to have to accept."

119

"Elle, you don't have to try to make me feel better." He reached up to remove my hand from his shirt, but I gripped it tight.

"You don't believe me?"

He raised an eyebrow and I went completely livid. I had told him he was hot to his face, and he was going to stand there and pretend I was lying to him.

Oh, hell no. That would not be happening.

I had admitted one of my biggest secrets, and by gosh, he would accept it. I glanced over and spotted Sloan standing on top of a table in the back corner, her eyes wide with excitement. She knew me too well.

Sure, I had some social anxiety. I normally didn't like people in general. There were certain people, though, special people who made this imaginary cut in my mind. Sloan and Ava were two of those people. Oliver had made the short list simply based on general perfection, but his kindness at volunteering to tutor me put him over the edge. That anxiety I felt when I imagined meeting him was gone. I no longer had to worry about whether or not this perfect guy I'd created in my head was a fantasy. Oliver was definitely real. In fact, he was better than the fantasy version, and I had to make him see that.

I smiled at Sloan. She was about to owe me five bucks for her ticket to the nerd show. I turned my attention back to Oliver. I slowly moved my hand from his shirt up to his neck and then tangled my fingers in his hair. It was softer than I expected.

"So naïve." I smiled and a confused look crossed

his faced. "Just so we're clear. This isn't to make you feel better. It's to satisfy my own obsession."

I clenched the fingers in his hair and the adrenaline coursed through me. I jerked his head down to mine and planted my lips directly upon his.

Such cool, soft, delicious lips.

I pulled him off balance and he was about to fall into me, so I pushed him backward, crashing through our chairs, until he finally hit the table. I took my free hand and shoved his hips up on the table, pushing him further back. I had to crawl up on the table myself to keep my lips on his. As I straddled him, I pulled his hair, leading his head down toward the table. I let my other hand snake its way through those brown locks, and then I pulled. Hard.

He gasped into my mouth, which was exactly what I wanted. I let my tongue slip in, tasting the sweet flavor of icing, and I reflexively ground myself up against him. That was when I felt his hands. Not on my face, shoulders, or back, but rather on my ass. Both of his hands gripped directly around my ass as he moaned into my mouth.

Oliver was trying to kill me.

Death by nerd. The new epidemic.

I flexed my fingers in his hair as I devoured his lips. Just call me Mufasa because Oliver was my innocent prey and I'd taken him down like an injured antelope. Then I remembered I was in the middle of the library. I needed to keep my control.

I gave him one last hard go around before I pulled back, ripping my lips from his. He gasped and followed me up. I scooted back off the table, admiring the view. His hair was in complete sex head disarray while he panted, trying to catch his breath. His hand moved up to straighten his glasses that sat off kilter on his face. I was about to tackle him again, library be damned, when I noticed about ten sets of eyes staring at us.

Nosy bastards.

Couldn't people have a good go at it in the middle of the library without attracting attention? I took one last long look at him before admitting that it would have to wait. I stepped up to my perfect nerd, letting myself stand between his legs. "Oliver Edwards," I said, with a stern tone as I ran my hand up his leg, "don't ever let me hear you doubt yourself again. You got that?"

He gaped at me, his chest heaving in air. I smiled. I leaned over, letting my hips rub against his thighs, and raked my finger through the icing on one of the cupcakes. I leaned back, placing the finger in my mouth, licking the icing onto my tongue. His eyes widened as I moved forward with my tongue still displaying the icing. He knew exactly what I was going to do because leaned in and graciously licked it off.

Oh, Oliver. Perfect naughty little Oliver. Did he realize who he was encouraging? He let out a whine as our tongues met and my hands gripped his thighs.

Pull away, Elle. Pull away.

There would be no nerd humping in the library. Well, at least in this section, anyway. Miraculously, I was able to unlock myself from his nerdy goodness for a second time. I pulled his hot little pouty lip out between my teeth as I enjoyed his taste combined with the icing. "Mmm." I grinned. "My new favorite flavor…strawberry Oliver."

He stared at me, licking his lips.

I pried my hands off his legs and stepped back. "We'll have to continue this anatomy lesson another day." I grabbed my backpack. "I hope you enjoy your cupcakes."

He sat there motionless as I smiled and walked off. My legs moved me in the opposite direction of where my body wanted to go, but I managed to defy it. I walked directly by Sloan, who still stood on top of the table, wide-eyed and open-mouthed. I gave a quick motion for her to follow me before gingerly passing her by.

I knew I would to have to go to the coffee shop and face my girls before going to work. Oh, how I wished I could just go home. I was about ready to say screw Sloan and my job and go home when I heard her high-pitched voice speeding up behind me. "Eloise Duncan! Slow your little nerd loving butt down."

I stopped as I came to the corner to cross the street in front of the coffee shop. "Yes, Sloan? Do you need something?" I asked innocently.

Her eyes were still the size of saucers, but I tried desperately to keep a straight face. "That—" she pointed back at the library, "—what the hell was that?"

I looked at her, confused, but then I couldn't hold in the smile. She busted out laughing.

"Get your butt in that coffee shop right now, young lady," she said, grabbing my shoulders, pulling me across the street. "I need details."

I allowed her to pull me inside, knowing there would be no escaping them today. Honestly, I wanted to relive it. I wanted to relive the last thirty minutes for the rest of my life. If only there was a thing as permanent life repeat. I would choose that moment. I'd choose every moment with Oliver Edwards.

Chapter Thirteen

INSPIRATION

I felt courageous. I would say almost to the point of daring and dangerous. I, Eloise Duncan, was a rebel. Did I sit around waiting for a boy to approach me? Hell, no. I stalked him, buttered him up with baked goods, knocked him in the nuts, and proceeded to seduce him in public, because that, my friends, was how that shit was done. At least, I slowly tried to convince myself that was true. If I was being honest, I should've probably been glad I wasn't in jail.

I sat smugly in the corner booth while Sloan wildly relayed a very detailed version of the events to Ava, who sat wide-eyed in complete shock. "Oh my gosh, Ava," Sloan continued in her usual frenzy, "she attacked him. Middle of the table, knocking chairs out of the way, straight out corrupted his nerdy soul."

Ava looked over at me, stunned. I shrugged like I was bored. You know, no big deal. I was smooth, confident, and skilled like that. Ava rubbed a hand down her face as she tried to process Sloan's story. "Did he like it? What did he do?"

I started to answer but Sloan interrupted me. "Are you kidding me? She could have baked him into a nerd pie and he would have died happily."

Ava smiled over at me. "Way to go, Elle. I have to say I'm impressed."

"Impressed?" Sloan scoffed. "I bow down to you, oh nerd goddess."

I let out a chuckle and rolled my eyes. "Okay, so are you two over this now?"

"Over it?" Sloan laughed, her eyes still wide and dancing. "I am officially inspired!"

She jerked herself around, eyeing Cowboy Joe behind the counter. She let out a purring sound as she snapped her teeth in his direction. I started to panic. "No, no, Sloan. Not in the middle of the coffee shop," I urged.

"Oh, you're one to talk," Ava said, giggling as she scooted up in her seat. "Sloan, I think this is an amazing idea. I totally support you."

"You haven't even heard what her idea is yet." I shot Ava a desperate look. I, as a former sideline girl, knew how to draw the line. I backed away from Oliver before we crossed that line between two crazy college kids, to making out weirdos on the evening news. Sloan had no such self-control. Sloan conquered. She would rule Preston and this coffee shop with the iron fist of public nudity.

I pointed at Sloan. "Do you see that crazed look in her eye right now?"

Ava looked to Sloan, who had Preston locked

126

into her sights. This wasn't good. This was going to end badly I could already tell. "Yep." Ava agreed, taking in my worried expression. "That is Sloan's 'I'm getting me some of that cowboy' look. I think she should go for it."

Preston chuckled at one of the customer's jokes as he dried off a coffee mug, and Sloan licked her lips.

"No, Sloan, don't." I reached for her across the table, but Ava wrapped her arms around me, holding me in my seat.

"Go, Sloan, go," Ava sang as an evil smile stretched across her face. "Show that cowboy how to really go down south."

Sloan shoved herself out of the seat, eyes still locked on her target. I pulled out of Ava's grasp, but Sloan was gone. "Damn it, Ava!"

"Give it up, Elle. She's going for it. There is nothing we can do but watch."

Sloan strutted toward the counter, her hoochie boots tapping against the tiled floor. She flung her hair over her shoulder. I could barely watch. No, actually, I couldn't look away.

"Well, hello there, Miss Sloan." Preston smiled innocently, sitting his mug on the counter.

"Hello...Joe."

Ava started slapping my leg with excitement. "She called him Joe. This is going to be good."

Preston gave her a strange look, but continued. "I didn't even see you come in. What can I get you today?"

That was about the time Sloan shoved the unsuspecting customer off the stool in front of him.

The guy looked like he was about to get pissed, but I think he realized the look on Sloan's face and decided it was in his best interest to back off.

"You want to know what you can get me today?" Sloan's voice sounded like a purr as she sat her knee up on the stool.

"Uhh, yes, Miss Sloan."

Oh, that poor boy. He didn't even see it coming. I squeezed Ava's shoulder as she bounced with pure giddiness next to me. "Sloan...Sloan," she chanted under her breath like it was the World Series of doing stupid crap.

Sloan was primed for attack with both knees on top of the stool, leaning over onto the counter. "You can get me one hot cowboy...to go."

His eyes widened and she pounced. Literally, pounced like a freaking puma, across the counter. One second she was there, and the next thing you knew, there was a loud commotion and they were both on the floor.

People in the shop gasped and a few stood, but Sloan and her prey were completely hidden by the tall counter. You could hear noises and groans. Ava and I practically sat in each other's lap trying to peer over for the tiniest of glimpses of what happened.

Soft murmurs erupted from around the shop, and I only prayed Sloan kept at least a portion of her senses in check. I didn't feel like bailing that idiot out of jail for public indecency today. Suddenly, two heads popped back up over the counter. Sloan grinned and Preston...well...Preston's expression looked very similar to one I had seen earlier today.

Shocked ecstasy? Sloan grabbed his belt buckle and pulled him forward. "Follow me, Joe."

He swallowed before throwing the rag he still had in his hand over his head. He didn't even bother looking back over his shoulder at their audience. He followed her toward the back room like a lost duck. As soon as they disappeared behind the closed door, the shop went completely silent. Well, completely silent except for the insane fit of laughter coming from Ava and me. Every eye in the place turned toward us, and we shut up. Ava nudged me. "Come on. Let's get the hell out of here."

I grabbed our stuff and ran for the door. As soon as we were outside, we busted out laughing again. "Did you see her go after him?" Ava imitated a cat-like pounce in the air, pretending as if she landed on her prey.

"Yes. That was priceless."

"Man, that makes me really sad I missed out on your nerd attack. I mean, that must have been some inspiration you gave her."

"I guess so." I giggled before glancing at my watch. I had to hurry or I would be late for work. "Look, if you talk to Sloan, tell her we have to meet for breakfast first thing in the morning. I need details, and maybe a pep talk before I go back to the library tomorrow."

"Sure. Sure." Ava continued to laugh, and I couldn't stop smiling. "We'll meet you in the morning."

I hurried to my car and rushed the last couple of blocks to Sugar Cube and managed to get there with five minutes to spare. Gretchen was in the kitchen, stacking a four-tier wedding cake. "Oh, my." I set my bag down on the counter. "Do you still have to decorate that monstrosity?"

Gretchen looked up, hopelessness in her eyes. Her normally perfect hair looked a little manic. "Yes. It's going to be a long night."

I grabbed my apron off the hook by the door. "What if I help? I can throw a batch of cupcakes in the oven, and I can decorate while they bake."

Gretchen sank with exhaustion against the counter. "You don't have to do that, Elle. Six dozen cupcakes is enough to keep you busy your whole shift."

"I want to help." And I meant it. Gretchen meant a lot to me. She sort of filled that spot in my life my mother left vacant. It was nice having someone you could bounce ideas off, and tell about your dreams without it immediately being followed by a lecture of why everything you want in life is wrong.

Gretchen stood and wiped her brow, smearing a smudge of icing across it. "I appreciate it. Thank you."

"It's not a problem. I'm happy to do it. Let me start my batter, and you can fill me up another bag of icing."

Gretchen and I worked diligently the next couple of hours. I baked my cupcakes and placed them in the freezer to cool down. Gretchen's wedding cake masterpiece had very intricate details. I carefully worked through the pattern inch by inch until we finally finished just before closing time. I wiped my palms on my apron. "I think it's done."

Gretchen stood back and admired the cake. "It's

perfect. I couldn't have done it without you."

I had to admit, I was pretty proud of myself. It was the first time I'd tried such a complicated pattern. It was relaxing. Therapeutic, almost. "Go ahead and cash out the register, and I'll put it in the freezer. I need to start my cupcakes."

Gretchen cleaned her hands. "You don't have to do that tonight. I'll finish them for you in the morning."

"No, that's okay. It won't take long to top them off, plus you have to deliver this cake tomorrow. It'll be fine."

Gretchen held up her hands. "All right. You don't have to twist my arm." She came over and gave me a hug. "I really do like having you around. I've never met anyone who likes this stuff as much as me."

I leaned into her hug. "I like being here. I'm pretty sure this job changed my life."

Gretchen squeezed me tighter. That was when I realized Gretchen had made my list of special people too. She saw the real me. She saw the potential trapped inside the struggling girl with the quirky fashion sense. She helped me flourish. The doorbell in the store dinged, and we both glanced at the clock. It was two minutes past closing time. Gretchen went out front, and I moved over to the door to see who it was. I shouldn't have been surprised, but I was.

Oliver Edwards.

He looked apologetically at Gretchen. "I know I'm late. I just need to make a quick request."

Amused, Gretchen grinned at him. "Okay, what

can I help with you with tonight?"

Oliver slipped his hands in the pockets of his jeans and rocked back on his heels. "I need to see Eloise."

Gretchen ran her hand decisively along the glass of the showcase while she walked toward the counter. "Is there any particular reason?"

"Not really." Oliver kind of smiled. "Other than the fact that I simply need to see her with my own two eyes."

Gretchen leaned over the counter. Oliver anxiously bit his lip. "Is she here?"

In my boss's defense, she at least thought about her answer first. "Let me go check."

Gretchen came in the kitchen, laughing. I'd backed all the way up into the closet as if that would somehow help me. My confidence from earlier today had somehow vanished without my consent. Gretchen noticed the terrified look on my face. "I'm assuming you heard that," she said, crossing her arms over her chest.

I nodded.

"Well," she said, waiting. "Are you here or not?"

I anxiously bit my fingernail on my thumb as I eyed the empty doorway. "It's complicated."

"How?"

"I don't know. I mean...I might have kissed him in the middle of the library earlier today."

Gretchen's eyes threatened to pop out. "You did what?"

I winced. "I told you it's complicated."

Gretchen moved closer to me. "I can't believe you spent the entire afternoon here with me and

132

didn't think it newsworthy enough to tell me you kissed your crush in the library today."

I shrugged. "I didn't think it was a boss kind of conversation."

Gretchen touched my shoulder. "I'm more than your boss, Eloise."

I knew that. I didn't know *she* knew that. "Okay," I said, shaking my hands as they started to clam up. "So, I kissed the boy I've been crushing on."

Gretchen ran her hands down her face. "Does he know it's you who has been leaving him the cupcakes?"

Again I winced. "No, but I fear that maybe he's figured it out."

"You fear?"

I threw my hands out as if it should be obvious. "Rejection is scary, or have you've forgotten the horrors of dating in your—"

She pointed her finger at me. "If you say old age, I swear, Eloise Duncan, I will invite that boy back here, right now."

I took a deep breath. "What should I do?"

"He came here to see you. See him."

I bit my lip. "Are you sure?"

Gretchen smiled. "I'm going to close up, and when I finish, I'm going out the front door to go home. You lock up when you're finished."

"You're going to leave us here…together…alone." I made it sound like Oliver was an ax murderer, but I couldn't help it. My confidence was so darn wishy-washy.

"Yes. I trust you." Then she gave me the mom

look. I didn't really know what a mom look was, but I imagined it looked like Gretchen. "I am very much trusting you to remember this is where I cook, and it should be treated with respect."

I nodded. Yeah, Gretchen was more than my boss. She knew me too well.

She took off her apron and hung it up on the hook by the door. "All right, then. I'll send him back."

I stood there in the door of the closet and I didn't move. Maybe I could turn into the invisible girl. Or I could fashion myself a fondant mask. I didn't know if I could simply stand here and let him see me. The *real* me.

Oliver appeared in the doorway of the kitchen. He had on a sky blue button down shirt with a pinstriped bow tie. He touched the edge of his glasses and smiled. "I knew it."

I forced out my own smile and stepped back out into the kitchen, twisting my fingers together behind my back. "How long did it take you to figure it out?"

He stepped a little closer to me. "I figured it out about the same time the blood flow went back to my brain."

I held out my hands, gesturing toward myself. "Surprise."

He didn't laugh. He didn't look freaked out or scared either. He simply cocked his head to the side. "Why didn't you tell me it was you?"

My hand found the counter to keep myself balanced. "It isn't obvious?"

He walked over to the other side of the counter.

That was smart to put something between us. Not that I couldn't climb that counter if I wanted. Sloan had proved without a doubt that you could perform such a feat. He leaned his elbows on it. "I'm a guy, Eloise. When is anything ever obvious to us?"

"I didn't tell you it was me because...well...I've been secretly gifting you cupcakes. It's a little embarrassing. That isn't something *normal* people do."

"You only did it because you overheard me, right? You heard me tell your boss how much I liked your cupcakes that day I came in here."

I twisted my lips. "Yes and no."

"What does that mean?"

"It means yes, I did overhear you telling Gretchen that you liked my cupcakes. But...I'd been aware of you for a lot longer than that."

He pushed his glasses up his nose, highlighting the ring of lush lashes around his perfect crystal blue eyes. "Aware of me?"

I took a deep breath. This was it. The confession. "You said you remember seeing me at the library a lot, right?"

"Well, yeah."

"I chose that seat for a reason. I was there all the time for a reason." I couldn't look at him. "It wasn't to study."

His brows pulled together like he was confused, but then it hit him. It hit him hard. He stood up straight. "You sat there because of me?"

I tucked my hair behind my ear. "What can I say? It was a nice view."

"Wow." He put his hand behind his head and

rubbed the back of his hair until it stuck out in all directions. "I have to say I'm a little flattered."

"Flattered is better than disgusted, I guess." I twirled my finger around in the flour on the counter.

Oliver lifted the edge of my chin, his face suddenly very serious. "Eloise. I feel like I should make my own admission."

I waited for him to continue. That hint of blush returned to his cheeks as he smiled. "I don't normally offer tutoring services to random people I meet in the library."

"I looked like I needed the help that much, huh?"

He grinned then walked around the counter to me. His hand touched my hair, his fingers running through it down to the twisty ends at my shoulder. "I've always been impressed with your dresses."

I looked down at the rose print on my dress. "Really?"

"If you were an icing flavor, you wouldn't be vanilla. You'd be the spice added to make everything else pop. You stand out in a crowd, that's for sure. Always so bright and colorful, yet somehow prim and proper. I was aware of you too, Eloise."

I laughed, trying not to let myself giggle excessively like a love-struck fool.

He leaned in a little closer. "Your hair always matches the style of your dress, and your lips are always red and shiny."

His gaze dropped to them. I knew because when I self-consciously licked them, he smiled. The timer on the counter dinged, and we both jumped. I grabbed it, and when I looked back, he'd stepped away a couple feet. I held up the timer. I wondered if he could see my disappointment. "It's time to decorate my cupcakes."

He perked up at the sound of that. "You mean I get to watch the master in action?"

"Sure, if you want to spend your night in a bakery with an oddly dressed, nerd-liking weirdo."

He touched my hip. His thumb ran over the blue bird there. "I do, actually."

I nodded toward the door. "Grab an apron. I could use an assistant."

Oliver put on an apron and washed up in the sink. I got a sleeve of cupcakes out of the freezer and grabbed a bag of my famous strawberry cheesecake icing. "Come here, let me show you how it's done." I placed a cupcake between us and iced the top perfectly in less than three seconds.

His eyes danced. "Wow. You've got skills."

I handed him the bag of icing. "Your turn."

He leaned back. "You don't want to sell something I decorate. Trust me."

I put the bag in his hands. "There are three extra...you know, for emergencies, in case I accidently drop one on the floor."

He held the bag of icing and stared at it. "Or if you lose your mind and let me decorate it."

"And that." I nudged his elbow. "Go ahead, give it a shot."

The sight of Oliver decorating a cupcake was indescribable. My two worlds clashing together. Why hadn't I thought of this before? He bit his lip, concentrating as he circled the top of the cupcake with the icing. It wasn't half bad. I wouldn't put it in my showcase, but I'd eat it. I walked up beside him and nodded. "Color me impressed. That's not bad for your first try."

He grinned down at his creation. "Thanks."

I pulled the pan of cupcakes over to me and easily started adding frosting to the top of each one in half the time it had taken him to do one corner. He watched me closely as I went one by one down the pan. After I finished, I motioned for him. "Could you add the sprinkles on top while I grab another tray out of the freezer?"

"Sure, that sounds like a task I can handle."

Oliver helped me finish up my orders. He applied toppings to all the cupcakes and assembled boxes. Honestly, I could have spent the entire night there working with him. He understood the need for the room to be quiet while I worked, but always managed to break the silence afterward with relative ease. Turned out I could add another adjective to the long list of things I loved about him.

Funny.

Oliver was witty and clever in a way I didn't realize guys could be. "So, where do you buy these dresses?" He bent down low to watch closely as he dropped the colorful sprinkles on top of the cupcakes I'd finished.

My cheeks lit on fire. So, he had really noticed my whimsical attire. "Different places. I find some online, and others at shops around town."

He stood back up straight and grinned at me. "What about those tights? There has to be a special kind of store where you get those."

I pointed my bag of icing at him. "Are you

teasing me?"

His grin was quick. "Yes. Is that a problem?"

I pressed my lips into a hard line to keep from smiling. "It will be if you keep it up. I promised my boss I'd keep this kitchen sanitary."

His lips quirked up at the edge as he ran his hand down the long side of the counter. "Well, that's a disappointment, now, isn't it?"

We both laughed, and I thought about bringing up the kiss in the library, but I didn't. This was too perfect. I took my time decorating the last of the batch, because I didn't want it to end.

When we finally finished, Oliver helped me close up the shop. He locked the door and pulled it shut. I looked down at my watch, rubbing the icing off the glass so I could see the time. It was past ten, which meant I would be up well past midnight trying to study for my quiz tomorrow night.

"What's wrong?"

I looked up to see Oliver watching me, his smile kind and worried. It made reality so much worse. That was what this was now…back to reality. Inside the library and the bake shop, I lived in a daydream. In there, I could pretend life and everything in it was perfect, that I had control over my own future. Out here, though, under the harsh light of the streetlamps, I couldn't deny the truth.

If I didn't pass my anatomy class with an acceptable grade, I would have to leave Maryland or lose the only parent I had left. Even if I passed, I couldn't tell my father about Oliver. He would find a way to keep me away from him. This buzz deep in my gut at the mere close proximity to Oliver would be nothing more than a memory I used to torture myself. "I would love to invite you over, but—"

"You need to study," Oliver guessed.

"I have a quiz tomorrow night."

Oliver walked me to my car. "I have some free time tomorrow, if you want to meet up and study again. I promise to try to rein in my cupcake lust long enough to keep our session on track this time."

I looked up at him, his perfect face all I could see. "Okay." I was going to fail. I was going to fail so bad. "Sure. Want to meet at ten?"

"Sounds good." He took his hands out of his pockets like he might do something with them, but then thought better of it and put them back. "I'll see you tomorrow."

"Oliver." I grabbed his arm.

His gaze came up to meet mine. I reached up and straightened his bow tie. "Thank you."

His brows scrunched together. "For what?"

I smiled and opened my car door. "For not running away screaming. I know I can be a little much to take in at first."

Oliver grabbed the door, blocking me in. "Eloise Duncan. I'm going to tell you this once, and only once." He leaned forward, placing his lips directly next to my ear, imitating the same tone I'd used on him earlier. His hand touched my waist, his thumb grazing over the polyester fabric of my dress like it was made of silk. "You're perfect. Strawberry cheesecake icing kind of perfect. Get used to it."

I sighed, and his forehead fell into mine.

My life was one huge, complicated mess.

Chapter Fourteen

POETRY

I stayed up to two a.m. studying, even though it felt more like memorizing my own death sentence. I would never need to use the information again, so I only needed to store it in my short-term memory long enough to pass the quiz, and then it could float away into some far corner of my mind never to be thought about again. I had much more important things to fill my permanent memory with now. All of them involved a certain tutor of mine.

My mind threatened to drift away into dreamland all morning, but I wanted to make sure I studied enough in case my study session with Oliver went astray somehow, then I would still manage to pass my quiz.

I had high plans on making the session go astray. There was something about the thought of getting Oliver back in the library, back in the same place where I'd kissed him yesterday, that made me want to repeat the process. Plus, I felt like there was this timer on our relationship and it steadily ticked down. If I wanted to enjoy my time with Oliver, I couldn't waste precious minutes.

I met Ava at the café for lunch, and we tracked down Sloan before her evening class. We found her skipping happily to her history class. Ava practically tackled her on the sidewalk before she could disappear into the building. "You've been ignoring my texts all morning."

Sloan wiggled her way out of Ava's hold with a wry smile. "I'm not ignoring you."

Ava put her hands on her hips. "What happened in that broom closet?"

"I told you last night." Sloan couldn't keep the gigantic smile off her face as she straightened her clothes. "I gave Preston my number and told him to call me."

Ava and I exchanged disbelieving stares that we then turned on Sloan. She attempted to keep a straight face, but it lasted about as long as a Disney star's abstinence vow. "Okay," she admitted, "I may have left my number on his butt."

Ava and I stopped walking. Sloan took a few more steps before she noticed we were missing and turned around. "What?"

Ava rubbed her head. "You left your number on his ass?"

"Yep." Sloan beamed with pride as if she'd just won the Nobel Peace Prize. "I mean, it seemed like a perfectly good spot."

I raised an eyebrow. "And cowboy was cool with that?"

She started giggling. "He didn't complain."

142

"That's it," Ava said, hopping between us, "Sloan has stolen your crown."

"For today maybe," I said, removing the container of cupcakes from my bag. I twirled them around in front of the girls. "Oliver showed up at Sugar Cube last night. He knows it's me who has been leaving him the cupcakes, so now I can indulge my nerd anytime I want."

Ava's eyes widened. "Are you going to see him right now?"

"We have a study session scheduled to start in ten minutes."

"But I have to go to class," Sloan said with a disappointed whine. "Can't you wait until later?"

"The boy needs his sugar fix," I explained. "I told him I'd meet him at ten, and I'm in the mood for some poetry."

Ava's eyes glazed over and sparkled. "Poetry."

Ava's sexcapades in the infamous secluded corner of the library were legendary. I patted her on the shoulder. "Exactly. So, I'm going take my cupcakes, and I will see you ladies later."

I trotted off in the direction of the library as Sloan's goodbye rang out over the quad. "Don't do anything I wouldn't do."

I sat silently working on my calculus homework, going over the problems I had already finished and checking for mistakes. Okay, who was I kidding? I was very impatiently waiting for Oliver to arrive. I wasn't hiding it very well at all. I scribbled on my paper, and my knee bounced all over the place. Eloise plus Oliver, minus clothes, multiplied by poetry section, divided by cupcake frosting, equaled all out schmexathon.

Fifteen minutes later, I was in full panic mode. No Oliver. No skinny jeans. No nerdy little glasses staring back at me. I had officially screwed things up. I thought we had a moment last night.

I wanted to kick myself. What the hell had I been thinking? You didn't try to defile a nerd in his sacred area. I had probably broken some unwritten nerd tribal law. No sexing on hallowed ground. Or maybe it was because I didn't invite him over last night. He'd made the grand gesture of showing up at my work, and stayed there helping me, all for what? I didn't even give him a hug goodnight.

There went that dream out the window. I guessed I just wasn't meant to stare into the gleam of those abnormally thick prescription lenses. I suddenly felt oddly empty inside. My life really did revolve around nothing more than getting an education now. There was nothing more to fill it with and pretend the classes and studying didn't exist. Seriously, who went to college just to get an education?

I could feel the sting of rejection welling up in my eyes. I supposed that's what you got for being bold and confident. They just left. They left you all alone in the middle of the library looking like a fool. Now that I thought about it, that had been exactly what I had done to him. So it fit. The tears spilled over, and I jumped up and ran for the bathroom. I threw the door open and ran for the sink. I bent my head and tried to calm the nausea. I squinted my eyes to squeeze out the remaining tears. I wanted it gone. I wanted it all gone.

Ten minutes later, my face was dry, my eyes red,

and I felt like got run over by the screw-you truck. I stumbled out of the bathroom toward my desk to gather up my things and go home. I would never go in a library ever again. I let out a long sigh and reached down to pick up my book.

My hand hit something hot. Something hot and a tiny bit gooey. I breathed in, and the smell consumed me. I knew that smell. I was a fan of that smell. My gaze shot down to my book to confirm what my nose had already told me. My hand sat on a gigantic plate of chocolate chip cookies.

Cookies. Glorious, hope-redeeming cookies.

Then I spotted a little blue folded paper sticking out from underneath the plate. I grabbed it, translating the chicken scratch scrawled upon it.

Made with appreciation for the cupcake queen.

P.S—I thought you were never going to get up and leave!

I choked back a chuckle as I read the last line. I bit my lip and picked up one of the cookies, biting off a chunk. They were delicious and I was an idiot.

"Elle?"

The whisper came from behind me and I let my head drop, soaking in the sound of my name in his rough voice. A cool hand gripped my hip, and then his body pressed up against mine. I instinctively leaned back against him. "I didn't mean to upset you," he whispered into my hair. "I thought I was being cute."

I smiled, turning around and burying my face in his flannel shirt. "It was. I simply have a flair for the dramatic."

He laughed into my hair. "How about next time I try to be cute, I give you fair warning?"

I looked up, taking in those magnified gorgeous eyes. "It would be greatly appreciated."

"Warning." His voice was deep and scratchy. "I'm going to kiss you."

My heart jumped in my throat and I swore that my panties hit the ground.

His lips caught mine and my knees went weak. His tongue raked across my lips. "Mmm. You taste like cookies."

I couldn't help but laugh. "You poor, food-deprived boy. I really am going to have to cook you that five-course meal."

His fingers played with the buttons on the star covered sweater I wore over my cotton candy colored sundress. "That sounds like a date."

"Because it is. Tomorrow night at my apartment at six."

His hands moved down to my hips. "Confession." He moved in closer, whispering between us. "I kind of like it when you tell me what to do."

It was funny how easily shy Elle faded away in Oliver's presence. He made me comfortable. Too comfortable. I reached up and touched his glasses. "Do you like poetry?"

Little sparks of lust burst from my fingertips. His nose scrunched up. "Is this some kind of test?"

I grinned. "No. I'm simply curious."

"Not really." He studied me warily. "But you can try to change my mind if you like."

I had to keep myself from purring the next sentence. "That is exactly what I was hoping you would say."

He looked confused as I grabbed his hand. "Bring the cookies and the cupcakes. You're about to receive your first poetry lesson."

I started walking backward, licking my lips at the thought. *Finally.*

He grabbed the goods and followed me. "Elle...should this be turning me on?"

I giggled and hooked my finger around one of the loops in his pants. I jerked him forward and placed a small lick on the edge of his ear. "You tell me."

I turned around, in a hurry to get him where we were going. Rushed footsteps echoed behind me.

"Uhhh...so where is the poetry section, exactly?"

The poetry section. That glorious little land of seclusion where young wild at heart youngsters could go to fulfill their greatest desires. This little filly's greatest desire was following her ever so eagerly toward that greatest of destinations. I practically skipped with delight, humming out my call to arms.

Top floor.

East Wing.

Left back corner.

Fourth row behind Custer's Last Stand.

Paradise.

I held my hands out, showcasing it to Oliver.

"So, this is the poetry section?" He glanced

around intently. He pulled a book off the shelf and opened it.

Only Oliver Edwards would look at a book in the flipping poetry section.

"Yes." I took the cupcakes and cookies away from him. I set them up on the table then unwrapped one cupcake and whistled toward Mr. Distracted. His eyes locked on the cupcake, and I knew I officially had his attention. He quickly put the book back and joined me on the table. "Hungry?"

He nodded. I placed the cupcake to his mouth, and he bit off a chunk. I strategically let the cupcake linger, smearing icing across his lips. "Oops." I grinned. "My bad."

He chuckled and leaned toward me. Oliver knew exactly how to play. I very slowly and methodically licked his lips clean.

"Damn, Elle."

"Shh." I held the cupcake back up. He sighed and took another bite.

We continued this sugary foreplay until there was only one tiny bite left. I ran my finger through the icing, and Oliver immediately opened his mouth.

"No, no." I grinned, shaking my finger at him. I ran my finger down my neck, spreading the icing down to my collarbone. "Come and get it."

Within seconds, his tongue was on my skin and I gasped. I hadn't expected him to react so quickly. My hand flew behind me for support, but I fell into the bookshelf with a loud thud. I suddenly became wary that someone might hear, but then I remembered Screamer Gonzales, AKA Ava "The Banshee" Morrison, had taught many a lesson in this corner.

His hands grasped my bottom, holding me in place, and I let out a little yelp of my own. He moaned as he licked against the icing, following the trail downward. His tongue snuck underneath the edge of my shirt, and he growled.

"This shirt," he said, keeping his voice steady, "is in my way."

This shirt could afford to be lost in the mountainous piles of melodramatic ramblings. Strippity-doo-da and the shirt was gone.

Dang, did he have fast hands. His fingers ran down the stretch of black lace along my bra as his lips devoured that mind numbing little spot between my shoulder and neck. "You taste…so good."

I thoroughly enjoyed being Oliver's little tasty treat, but my own hunger needed to be tamed. I unlocked my legs, dropping to the floor. I pulled Oliver down with me. I shoved his shoulders up against the back of the shelf, ripping apart the buttons of his flannel shirt one by one.

This little button went to the library.

Snap.

This little button stayed home.

Snap.

This little button had cupcakes.

Snap.

This little button had none.

I snatched his shirt open, moaning to myself as my hands ran down his bare chest. Now there was only one button left that I cared about. My hand dropped down to his jeans.

This little button cried "this is happening now" all…

Zip.

The way.

Zip.

Home.

Red cotton briefs stared up at me. Inches stood between my fingers and the road to glory. I pulled his pants apart, panting with excitement.

A strong hand caught my shoulder, and I raised my gaze to Oliver, who looked like he was about to have a panic attack. "You sure about this?"

"You promised me an anatomy lesson." I ran my finger along the line of his boxers, eliciting sharp, curt breaths. "Are you backing out on me?"

He watched my hand trace around the edge, and he finally shook his head.

"Good."

He raised his gaze to me, his entire body frozen in place. My fingers dipped below the edge of the fabric as he watched, motionless. "So, what lesson shall we start with?"

A low rumbling built in his chest. I touched his lips. "Hmm, this one, maybe?"

He shook his head.

I moved lower to his neck. "This one?"

I grazed his collarbone, adding pressure. "No."

"Then show me."

He pulled my lips to him. His kiss was more urgent this time. Desperate, almost. Daring and unspeakable things started coming to my mind. Things even Sloan wouldn't do in the poetry

150

section.

"Elle?"

"Hmm?"

"I've got your first assignment ready."

I pulled back slightly to see his tortured face. "Oh, really?"

A dark, lust-filled smirk spread across his lips as he pushed his glasses up. "I'll even give you extra credit if you don't make me explain the instructions."

I laughed, lowering my lips back to him. "I think I can handle that."

I pulled his pants down and noticed his eyes glancing behind us. "No one will hear us," I assured him, not bothering to take my attention off the task at hand.

"Just nervous. I've never done this." He took a quick breath. "I mean...not in a library."

"Me either." I smiled up at him. "Let me take your mind off it."

I gripped the cotton and jerked. Hard. It felt so good. It was like ripping open a Christmas present, but better. This present I would never get tired of, though.

His entire body stiffened and his mouth opened, but no words or air came out. I knew how he felt. Dazed. I couldn't believe it either. I had Oliver...naked...in the library.

I crawled on top of him, kissing him into submission. Oliver started mumbling in a language I didn't understand. It wasn't until his fourth time through this process I caught on to exactly what he said.

"Bromine, mercury, hydrogen, helium."

He recited the periodic table, except he wasn't doing it backward. Instead, he was doing it by elemental category—liquids, gases, and solids. That was the last freaking straw. This nerd was mine.

I stepped back long enough to slip my panties off underneath my dress, and he started reciting louder. "Nitrogen, oxygen, fluorine." I threw them at his face. "Ne—on."

I moved back down to him, smiling to find my red lipstick smeared across his lips. I planned to kiss him again, but not there.

"Holy shit." His hands found my hair as my lips found him. After that, it was only a matter of time. Well, more like a matter of seconds. Normally, I would giggle at his quick reaction, but the poetry section tended to have that kind of effect of guys. Oliver hadn't stood a chance.

His body trembled, and I felt his fingers tracing the line of my back. He mumbled something I couldn't understand again, but he smiled, so I knew it was fine. He sat up, panting with wide eyes and flushed cheeks.

I smirked at him. "Do I pass?"

"I think you just took my job." He ran his fingers through his hair and took in a deep breath.

"Then maybe I'll give you homework next time." I would teach him control. He'd be my little gifted experiment. "And in case you have any questions, Mr. Edwards."

I had planned this part out ahead of time. Sloan was not about to outdo me. I reached over and pulled the Sharpie out of my backpack. Then I jerked his hip around. I scribbled my number across his glorious *gluteus maximus*. Of course, that would be the body part I remembered.

"Next time?" He looked down, trying to watch me as I applied my phone number to his skin. "Not next time."

Now it was my turn to be confused. He pulled his pants up, but didn't bother to fasten them. Instead he pulled me to him and rolled me over. "I was thinking more like right now."

My breath shook along with my vagina. Right now? Like, right freaking now? He started running kisses down my chest while I busied myself tangling my fingers in his hair. It wasn't like I could make it any messier than it already was. He hovered around the hem of my bra, nipping at the lace and driving me freaking insane. Right now was definitely a good time.

A loud knock echoed on the other side of the shelf, then a burst of giggles rang out, followed by a heavy slap against bare skin. "Ava. Hush."

Oliver's gaze immediately flashed up to mine, and he panicked. That would have been the completely normal reaction if I hadn't known exactly who our intruders were. He quickly zipped up his pants and grabbed his shirt. "Elle. Someone is here!"

"Yes, and they are about to get their asses kicked." I stood and straightened my skirt. "Ava. Sloan. Get on this side of this bookshelf right now."

Oliver handed me my shirt as my two best friends slowly peeked their heads around the corner, looking guilty as hell. Sloan's face was contorted into a complete grimace. "Sorry. We were trying to be quiet."

"Sloan." My teeth were locked together as my frustration leaked out.

Oliver looked between us. "Oh, wow. These are your friends."

I slid my shirt on and nodded. "My stupid, nosy friends who don't know how to mind their own business."

Ava threw on her pageant smile. "Yes, and you must be Oliver."

His cheeks flushed and he held out his hand. "Uh, yeah, I'm Oliver Edwards. Nice to meet you both."

Ava started to grab his hand, but Sloan caught her and pulled it back. "Don't touch that. We don't know exactly where it's been," she said, examining his fingers. "We could only hear over there. We couldn't see anything."

Oliver looked at his outstretched hand, confused.

I glared at her, and you could almost see the evil twinkle in her eyes. It simply screamed "Payback." Hadn't she paid me back enough with that stupid little poem she wrote? Oliver's face went white. "Oh no, what time is it?"

Sloan glanced down at her watch. "Eleven thirty."

"Shit, I'm going to be late for class." He whipped himself around to me and buttoned up his shirt.

He strategically turned so only I could see his face. "Can we umm…finish this later?"

I smiled, running my hand over his ass. "Call

me. You've got my number."

He bit back a smile. "Is that what you wrote?"

I nodded, and he closed his eyes, grinning. "Talk to you soon, then." He turned, gathered up his cupcakes, and gave the girls a wave goodbye. Of course he didn't forget the cupcakes.

I waited until he was out of hearing distance before I turned my wrath on them. "What the hell?"

"Sorry," they squeaked in unison.

Sloan clasped her hands as if begging. "I'll make it up to you."

I smacked Ava's hand as she reached for a cookie. "Don't you dare. You think you get an Oliver cookie after that?"

She pouted. "Fine. Will you at least still come to the baseball game tomorrow?"

I grabbed my cookies and stuffed one in my mouth. "Yes. You are both buying me hot chocolate and popcorn or anything else I want. Maybe for the next year, but definitely tomorrow."

I stomped off to go find my books and attempt to go to class. I glanced down at my poor deprived vagina. It was times like these I was glad I was female. At least the whole world couldn't see its disappointment.

Chapter Fifteen

RAIN

I held my anatomy quiz out in front of me, grinning at the red ninety-three on the top. I didn't just pass the quiz, I passed it with an A! Unfortunately for me, quizzes weren't worth as much as the midterm exam, so I needed a lot of A quizzes to bring my grade back up to an acceptable range, plus an awesome final exam grade. Tonight was a small step in the right direction, though.

I sat on the concrete steps leading out of the science building and smiled down at the paper. This bad boy was going on my fridge. A streak of lightning flashed across the sky, and I didn't even care. Let it rain. Let a monsoon unleash its fury on me. I wouldn't care. Not right now. Nothing could take away the pleasure and satisfaction of this small accomplishment. A couple drops of rain sprinkled on my head, and I frowned up at the dark night sky. Thunder rumbled back at me.

I reluctantly pulled myself up to start the seven-block walk to my apartment, when the sprinkle turned into an outright spring rainstorm. I pulled my jacket off and held it over my head. I ran all the way across campus, splashing through puddles. My shoes were soaked, and the wind blew the rain underneath my jacket. I found sanctuary under the ledge leading into the student services building. I threw my jacket on the ground and wiggled water off myself like a wet dog. The thunder continued to rumble above my head, and another flash of lightning streaked across the sky.

Maybe I was wrong about the monsoon. It might deter my good mood a little bit at this point.

I got my phone out to check the weather, hoping this would only be a short storm and I could impatiently wait it out before going home. I clicked my phone on only to realize I'd missed another call from my dad. I should probably call and at least leave a message with his secretary tomorrow. Maybe it would get him off my back for a few days.

The weather report said my wait would be at least an hour. That totally killed my mood. I couldn't stand around and wait an hour for the rain to let up. I clicked my cell screen off, prepared to face the storm head on. Then the screen lit up again and my familiar 90s pop ring tone blared out. I almost ignored it, thinking it was only my dad again. I didn't recognize the number, though, or the location. Who did I know from Augustus, Maine?

I let it go to voicemail, convincing myself it was probably a wrong number. Just as I was about to stuff it into my backpack, the screen lit up with a text from the same number.

Unknown: Hey. It's Oliver. Just checking on the verdict of your quiz. Good? Bad? Eat an entire tub of rocky road ugly? Let me know how it went.

I smiled.

Oliver was thinking about me. It must be all the sugar I fed him. He was too sweet.

I called him back as I attempted to tame the mass of wet hair that fell into my eyes. He picked up on the first ring. "Eloise?"

That voice. My good mood was instantly restored. I smiled against the screen of my phone. "I made an A."

Oliver sighed deeply on the other end. "That's great."

"I appreciate the rocky road suggestion, though. If I end up failing the class, I'll take you up on that."

"You're not going to fail. I won't let you."

I thought about admitting everything that was on the line, but I didn't want to think about it. "I appreciate that. It at least gives me hope."

"We should celebrate," he said, and I could picture his sweet smile. "Where are you?"

"I'm stuck underneath the overhang at the student services building."

He paused. "What do you mean stuck?"

"Do you not hear the storm?" I held the phone out so he could hear the thunder. "I have to walk seven blocks in this mess."

"No, don't do that. Stay there. I'll come get you."

"You don't have to do that—"

"It's not a problem. I just got out of class too. I'm only a couple buildings away."

I turned around to the large window of the building and frantically started trying to straighten out my wet dress and comb through my crazy hair.

"Stay put," he said. "I'll see you in a minute."

I put my phone back in backpack and scowled at my reflection in the glass. My hair looked like something from the walk of shame hall of fame, but it was too late to worry about it. Oliver walked toward me in the distance. I could see him because of the street lamp down the sidewalk. He held a giant umbrella and smiled like he knew it. He gave it a slight twirl, causing the rain to pelt off it in all directions. He stood beneath it, perfectly dry and smug.

I smiled sweetly at him. "My hero."

He eyed my soaked state and frowned a little. "I think I might be a little late for that."

As he stepped closer, I noticed something different about his umbrella. In the dim light it took me a moment to realize what looked different about it. I picked up my bag, still staring at it. "Your umbrella," I said, pointing at it. "Is it also a lightsaber?"

Oliver grinned. "Noticed that, huh?"

He took his finger and flipped a switch at the chrome metal base of the handle, and the shaft of the umbrella lit up a perfect Luke Skywalker blue. "It makes a nice flashlight."

I laughed. Oliver was nerd utopia. "That is awesome."

"Really? Is that why you're laughing?"

I tried to hide my smile with my hand. "I'm not making fun of you. It's just—here you are, standing in front of me with your cute little glasses and sexy bed hair, holding your Star Wars umbrella while offering to walk me seven blocks to my apartment to keep me out of the rain. I'm scared I've finally lost it and my brain has completely made you up."

Oliver held out his hand. "I'm real, Eloise. I promise."

I threw my backpack across my shoulders and ran to him. I took his hand, and he pulled me into his side. I poked him in the chest. "I'm still debating it."

He held me close to his side, keeping me under the safety of the nylon as we ventured down the sidewalk. "My apartment is that way," I said, pointing toward the north end of campus. "I live in the apartments down past Sugar Cube."

"I'm familiar with the area. Is it the white ones on the corner or the brick apartments with the calico cat that always sits out front?"

"The brick ones and the cat…his name is Peter Pan."

Oliver cocked his head. "I always thought he was a stray."

"He is, but even strays deserve a name. He frequents the alley behind Sugar Cube. I sneak him scraps on my breaks."

"Do you feed all the stray, starving souls in the city, or just me and Peter Pan?"

"Just the two of you so far."

He knocked his hip into mine. "Good. I was

about to get jealous."

As we made our way off campus, the rain didn't let up, which was fine by me. I enjoyed the close confines of the umbrella. His fingers never left my hip. I could feel each individual one of them pressing against the fabric. Oliver peered down at me. "I'm glad to hear about your grade. Would it be too presumptuous to say we make our study dates a weekly thing?"

"The study sessions or the trip to the poetry section?"

Oliver looked out at the rain in front of us and grinned. "Both?"

Euphoria consumed me at the thought. "I think that would be a perfectly appropriate amount of presumptuousness."

"Good, because I already added it to my to-do list."

We hurried across the street before the crosswalk could stop us. My foot landed in a puddle that turned out to be a lot deeper than it looked. Water splashed up my dress and I squealed. Once we made it to the other side of the street, I stopped and danced around a little. That was really cold. Oliver laughed behind me. "I bet you're really missing your underwear right about now."

I shot a glare over my shoulder at him. I thought I was the only one who knew I'd forgotten to pick up my panties off the library floor after Sloan and Ava interrupted us. Apparently, Oliver had noticed too. I'd never gone commando before, and it had been awkwardly annoying all day. If felt like everyone knew, even if they had no way of knowing. "Yes, underwear would have been nice right now. I suspect those are lost forever."

"Well...actually..." Oliver held his umbrella with one hand and used the other to pull a pair of pink, all too familiar undies out of his front pocket.

I gasped. "Oh my gosh. Are those mine?"

Oliver rolled his eyes. "No. They're mine. I just keep a pair in my pocket for emergencies."

I snatched them from him, and he looked sheepishly down at me. "I grabbed them while we were hurrying to get dressed. I didn't want some random janitor to find them, but I got in a hurry and ran off with them."

I eyed him curiously. "So, you've been walking around all day with my underwear in your pocket?"

He smirked. "Maybe."

I bit my lip and playfully swatted at him. "Pervert."

He shrugged. "Better me than some random guy you haven't seduced with your sugary confections, though, right?"

"Seduced?" I acted as if this accusation shocked me. "Is that what you think I was doing when I gave you cupcakes?"

He leaned down to whisper in my ear. "A guy can hope."

He took my hand, and I moved back into his side as we started walking again. I slid my underwear in my jacket pocket. We made it half a block, and Oliver paused outside one of the fancy high-rise apartment complexes that sat just off campus. "Do you mind if we stop by my place for a second? I need to let my dog out."

I stopped mid-step. "Wait. You live here?"

I glanced up at the tall, obviously new building with its untarnished bricks and modern architecture. "Technically, yes." He motioned toward the front door. "Do you mind?"

"No, of course not. Beggars can't be choosers, right?"

I followed him up to his apartment, my mouth gaping the entire way. The building definitely didn't look like something a college student could afford. Ever. Oliver lived on the top floor in the freaking penthouse, of all places. There was something definitely fishy about that. My apartment could fit in the elevator of this place. He unlocked the door, and as soon as he twisted the knob, a large, shadowy figure darted out the front door toward him. Oliver stumbled back a couple feet, and it was only then I realized the dark figure was his dog. A giant black lab jumped up and down in an attempt to reach Oliver's face with his slobbery tongue. Oliver tried to keep the dog down. "Yes, I know, Scuba. I'm happy to see you too."

Oliver scratched the dog's ears and patted his head affectionately. Oliver looked over at me and smiled. "Scuba here isn't used to apartment living yet. He doesn't understand why he isn't out on the boat every day."

"The boat?"

Please, tell me he didn't own a yacht. I didn't think I could date a guy with a yacht.

"My parents, they own a fish hatchery off the coast up north. Scuba would go out with me and my dad every day on our boat and help bring in the catch."

"Ah. That's right. You're from Maine. That's what your number showed up as on my caller ID."

Oliver led me into his apartment, or mansion, whatever you wanted to call it, and threw his keys on the table by the door. "Yeah. I've lived there all my life until I was shipped off to college."

My head turned toward the side. "Shipped off?"

"Ah, well, I guess I shouldn't say it like that. My parents...they were very adamant about making sure I got the college experience. They've had it hard making a living, and they just want to make sure my life is easier. They can be a little overbearing about it."

Now I was really confused. If his parents weren't rolling in the dough, then how the heck did he afford this apartment?

Scuba scarfed down his bowl of food while Oliver grabbed his leash off the top of the fridge. The gesture pulled his shirt up, and I saw a hint of the creamy flesh beneath. More specifically, his amazingly toned body. "So, you helped your dad out on his boat. I guess that explains the mystery of your abs."

Oliver turned around. "My abs?"

"You have very nice abs for a guy who spends a lot of time in a library studying. Now it makes sense."

Oliver bit the inside of his cheek. "Do you play a game to see how many times you can get me to blush in one day?"

I smirked, unrepentant. "Yes."

We shared a smile as he walked over and hooked

Scuba up to his leash. "Do you care if we both escort you the rest of the way home? He could really use a long walk."

I walked over and gave Scuba a pat on the head. He licked my hand before scarfing down the remainder of his snack. "Does he get embarrassed easily? Because I'm going to kiss my Jedi hero goodnight."

Oliver blushed for the third time, because he was totally right. I kept count.

"Maybe, but he'll survive it."

Oliver and Scuba walked me home underneath the blue glow of his umbrella. Even with my tangled hair, wet feet, and bare bottom, it was a perfect night. Now I just had to make sure I made the grade to keep these perfect nights a possibility.

Chapter Sixteen

JOCK

Sloan bought me three cups of hot chocolate at the game Saturday. The guilt was strong with that one. As it should have been after they so rudely interrupted my poetry time with Oliver. I didn't go knock on the broom closet door after she dragged Preston out of the coffee shop. My friends needed to learn boundaries. The major boundary being not to interrupt any kind of alone time I had with Oliver, especially if they found us in the poetry section.

Ava had yet to buy me a cup, but she was currently busy. By busy, I meant she straddled the railing of the outfield, whining like a cat in heat while she watched Brad and his teammates warm up for their game. "It's not fair. I can't tackle Brad on the baseball field. People make the evening news for that kind of craziness."

I took a gulp of my hot chocolate, giggling. I wasn't going to lie. It felt good to be making progress with Oliver while watching Ava suffer a little. Usually, I was the one who got left walking home from the bar alone because Ava had met some guy and bailed on me. I wanted Ava to succeed in her pursuit of Brad, but it felt good to finally beat her to the punch for once. "You'll have to find a different place to pounce him," Sloan suggested, casually offering me some nachos.

I took them, smiling appreciatively. Sloan earned brownie points like a boss.

Ava turned around. Her eyes narrowed at both of us. "I've tried. I can't find one single place that boy hangs out other than this stupid baseball field. I've been at Rowdy Randy's every weekend for weeks, and nothing."

I crunched down on my nacho. "How about the locker room?"

Sloan laughed, propping her feet up on the railing in front of us. "You can't break into a locker room."

I rolled my eyes. "It's not breaking in if you get lost. People make mistakes all the time."

"That's not a half bad idea." Ava's eyes widened and she jumped off the railing, running over to me. "Oh, Elle, please come get lost in the locker room with me. Please. Please. Please."

I took another sip of my drink, glancing over at Sloan. I wouldn't do it without her. Sloan shrugged. "I'll get arrested if you will."

I turned back to Ava, who had her hands fisted around the arm of my seat. "You owe me hot chocolate."

She practically tackled me. "Oh, thank you so much, Elle. I will owe you forever!"

"Damn right, you will," I said, throwing back my last drink. "And both of you will never interfere in my alone time with Oliver ever again."

"Never." She hugged me to pieces. "I promise."

"All right. All right." I pushed her off and leaned over to take more nachos from Sloan. "We shall help you land your jock today."

The game took forever, or at least it felt that way with Ava babbling on and on about what she might say or do once she made her way inside the locker room. Ava was never patient or subtle when it came to guys, and it didn't matter how much Sloan and I tried to convince her to take it a little slower. It was all or nothing with her all the time. We finally learned to live with it.

We waited by the bathroom, pretending to have some in depth conversation about a fictional heartthrob we all knew while everyone filed out of the stadium after the game. The walkway became heavily crowded, so we slowly made our way toward the back corner. Once we got past the crowd, we had to go into stealth mode. Suddenly the "Mission Impossible" theme song started playing through my head. We hid behind columns, peeked around corners, and bolted down a staircase clearly marked **"Players and Employees Only."**

At the edge of the stairs, I stopped and carefully glanced around the corner. Players and coaches filed out of the locker room carrying their bags and slinging the water off their wet hair. I held up my hand, signaling for them to wait. Ava climbed up on my back, trying to peer around the corner, but I managed to shake her off. "Would you please be patient? You're going to get us caught."

The horde of people finally slowed down, and Ava pushed against my back. "Hurry or we will miss him."

"We won't miss him, idiot." I tried to push her back. "He'll be the last one out."

"How do you know that?"

"He's the star player, Ava. I'm sure he had to do a ton of interviews after the game, which means he'll be the last one to leave. "

It had been about five minutes, and no one had emerged, so I gave Ava the go-ahead. We walked down the hall pretending to be thoroughly confused and one by one backed our way through the locker room door. Once inside, the room opened into a giant empty space. Large, navy blue lockers outlined the walls of the room, and the floor was littered with towels, socks, and other smelly, weird things I didn't feel the need to inspect. Ava looked around, disappointed. "He's gone."

A noise erupted behind us. We all three jumped. Technically, Ava and Sloan jumped at me as if I was some grand protector. Little did they know I was about to hightail it out of there and leave them for dead. However, that wasn't necessary, and I shoved them off me. "It's the shower," I said as quietly as possible. "He turned on the shower."

Ava's eyes lit up like she'd seen the Holy Grail.

"No, Ava. We are not busting in on somebody in the shower."

"But, Elle," she said bouncing up and down, "he's all wet and naked in there."

I pointed my finger at her. "No."

Somebody had to keep her under control. Ava was too much like Sloan. She had no boundaries or fear of consequences. She snarled at me before turning to the lockers. She ran her hand down the sides, inspecting the name plates above each one. Surprise, surprise whose she stopped at. The door was cracked, with a pair of shorts hanging off the edge. She slid her hand along the edge, opening it. Her other hand darted inside, pulling out a piece of clothing. She smirked as she held them up. A pair of skimpy Under Armour undies. She stretched them out, watching them contract. "Oh, can you just imagine?"

Sloan eyed them warily. "How the hell does he fit all of that in those little things?"

"I will find out," Ava vowed, "and I will report back."

The water suddenly cut off, replaced by a loud, booming voice, singing. We panicked. Ava slung the shorts up in the air, and we started frantically turning in circles searching for a place to hide. I let out a very frantic, yet silent squeal of terror. I hastily started jerking down locker handles like they were the zipper on Oliver's pants.

Locked. *Shit.*

Locked. *Damn it.*

Locked. *Mother chucker.*

Click.

I jerked the door open. It looked spacious enough. Sloan was the nearest to me, so I grabbed her and shoved her in. I followed after her. Ava tried to stick her foot in, but she wouldn't fit. "Try a different locker."

The vibrant voice continued to sing on the other side of the corner. I mouthed "sorry" and shut the door in Ava's horrified face. That was what she got for not buying me hot chocolate. She cursed me under her breath before the singing suddenly cut off. There was silence for about five seconds before I heard a very familiar yet explicit seductive voice. "Oh, well...hello, Brad."

"Umm, hello," Brad stuttered.

I tried to crane down and place my ear to the edge of the slit in the door to hear better, but there was no room to budge. Not to mention it smelled liked rotten jock straps. Sloan managed to bring her fingers up and clamp her nose off.

"I'm Ava," she cooed, still laying on the charm.

"Yeah, I remember. You do know you're in the guys' locker room, right?"

"Huh? Really? I had no idea."

That a girl, Ava. Play dumb.

Sloan giggled, and I jabbed her in the ribs. Ava's voice got smoother with a hint of a pout. "I got separated from my friends on the way out of the stadium, and I got lost."

"Well, that wasn't very nice of them to go off and leave you," Brad said, letting out a laugh.

"Yeah, they are quite inconsiderate."

I could only imagine the bitch-fest she was having at my expense in her head right now.

There was silence again, and I struggled to bend down. I shoved Sloan and she hit me back, but I managed to maneuver low enough to peek through the top slit. I saw flesh and a bright white towel. "I'm not interrupting anything, am I?" Ava asked innocently.

"No," he blurted out, but quickly regained his composure. "I was just taking a shower."

"And I missed it?" Ava giggled and her ass blocked the view of Brad's white towel.

I slapped Sloan in the side. "Holy crap. She's going for it."

"For what?"

"The towel."

A few more mumbling sounds chatted back and forth that I couldn't make out, and the next thing I knew, a blur of white fabric headed for my face. The towel hit the outside of our locker, and Sloan gasped with a huge smile on her face.

Bow chica wow wow.

Sloan and I tried desperately to hold in our giggles as a moan erupted from the outside. I bent back down, and Ava had Brad pinned down on top of a bench...butt naked.

Sloan nudged me with her knee. "What's happening?"

"I think she is going for the home run, Sloan. Ava isn't playing games out there."

If I could have seen Sloan's face, I knew she would be rolling her eyes right now. "Just like her," Sloan said. "She never learned how to run the bases."

I peeked out and instantly wished I hadn't. Stark white flesh headed our way. I quickly cupped my hand over Sloan's mouth, just in time for the impact. Sloan screamed into my palm as Ava's backside slammed into the locker. How had Brad stripped her clothes off that fast?

Psht. Who was I kidding? This was Ava. She probably went commando every day.

I removed my hand from Sloan's mouth as she gasped at me in horror. The moans were definitely a lot louder and more distinct now.

Sloan gave me an 'oh no, he isn't' look, but then it started. The pounding. I thought the locker was going to cave in. Sloan and I grabbed each other, sinking away from the door as much as possible as Ava's ass slammed into it over and over again.

If that wasn't bad enough, my phone vibrated in my pocket. Sloan felt it on her leg and practically dismantled the inside of the locker before she figured it was only my phone. Luckily Brad was distracted out there, or I was sure he would have heard that one.

I slid the phone out of my pocket, attempting to get a look at the number. It wasn't local, but it wasn't a number in my contact list. It was Oliver.

Shit.

I couldn't answer it right now. Not with the McFreaksters going at it on the outside of the door. Sloan silently yelled at me to answer it. I glanced toward the number and then back at the imploding door.

Double shit.

"Hello," I whispered into the receiver the same the time Ava let out a scream.

"Uhhh…Elle?"

"Yes?"

"This is Oliver." There was a long pause. "What the heck is going on in the background?"

"Um." I glanced at Sloan, who urged me with

her eyes. "Sloan is working out. She's a screamer."

"Okay." Another awkward pause. "I'll take your word for it. I was calling to see if you wanted to get together later. I know we have study dates scheduled, but I wanted to ask you out on an official first date."

There was a loud boom on the outside of the door, and it literally bent inward. Sloan nearly shrieked. "Sounds great, Oliver. How about you come to my house around eight?"

"Okay, sounds good. See you then."

I quickly shut off the phone as glass-shattering shrieks of pleasures rang out. Well, at least the pounding had stopped. It got quiet after that except for the heavy panting. I tried to calm Sloan down, but she kept acting like R. Kelly was trying to break into her closet. There was light mumbling outside the door, but I didn't bother to try and listen. I wasn't in the mood to hear Ava's acceptance speech for freak of the week.

I waited five minutes before even attempting to take a peek outside. When I did, Brad stood next to his locker, wearing that stretchy contraption he called boxers. He'd fit it all in, surprisingly, but it sure didn't leave anything to the imagination. I had the sudden urge to get the hell out of this stink hole. Luckily, Ava lured Brad out of the room within minutes.

We busted open the door, gasping for fresh air. Sloan heaved it in like it was the last breath she would ever get to take. "It's official," Sloan said, panting between words, "we have got to start talking to guys in bars like normal people."

I nodded in agreement as I tried to fan the stink away from me. "A flat surface and some sheets have never sounded better."

I pulled her outside, sneaking out a back exit. We rounded our way to the parking lot, expecting to see Ava waiting for us at the car, but she wasn't there. Instead, she lay on the hood of a black Cadillac about two hundred yards in the distance with Mount Brad hovering over her.

She could find her own way home. I jumped in the car, and Sloan quickly followed. I had a date to prepare for, and, well, horrible images to scrape out of my brain.

Chapter Seventeen

FANGS

I, Eloise the Magnificent, had a plan. My first plan of seducing Oliver with cupcakes had worked like a charm, so I thought, why not try out another one? I was good with plans. I was a very detailed oriented kind of gal, which made my plans all the greater. This particular plan was full of details. I had it broken down into stages. Accomplishing minor tasks helped build up to accomplishing the overall goal. The goal being getting nerdy beefcake between my sheets tonight. Oliver could have his own plans, for all I knew. When I sent him a text to confirm the time, he simply replied with a

"see ya then, cupcake."

So, I officially had no clue as to what his intentions were for the evening, but I knew very well about mine.

Stage One: Sex up my style.

I was pretty well-known for rocking the quirky girl look, but I could be a vixen when I wanted. I too owned a pair of hoochie boots. I simply chose not to unleash them on every random soul walking down the street like Sloan. I enjoyed the element of surprise.

Stage two: Butter Oliver up with food.

That was a given. If it wasn't not broke, don't fix it, right? I would have him eating out of my hand or off my body, one way or another. That would essentially lead straight into stage three.

The doorbell rang, and I practically jumped out of my panties. I took one last look in the mirror.

Sexy, low cut black sweater.

Check.

Butt cleavage leather mini.

Check.

I swung the door open, thirsting to see my nerdilicious perfection. I squeezed my legs together and bit my lip in preparation before throwing the door open.

"Hello, Elle."

I stood there. I just stood there. In the place of my oh-so-perfect nerd stood...a cowboy. I was so confused. It was definitely Oliver. His piercing blue eyes still bored into me as he ran his fingers through those soft brown locks. However, there were no skinny jeans, and most importantly, there were no black-rimmed glasses. Instead there were blue jeans, a plaid shirt, and boots.

Cowboy boots.

I blinked. Something had gone terribly wrong. Had it finally happened? Had Sloan taken over the

177

world and followed through on her threat to pass a "cowboy all day every day" law?

He noticed my utter confusion and smirked at me. Did he think this was some kind of joke? Because it wasn't funny.

It was not funny *at all*.

"Elle," he said, smiling at my expression, "I can explain."

I waited with my hands on my hips. There had better be a damn good excuse for this tragedy. "I would have told you earlier on the phone, but you seemed rather busy." He leaned up against the doorframe and smiled like he was a genius. "Would you attend a party with me tonight? A costume party?"

A costume. A costume party. Oh, thank god. Oh goodness, thank you. It was only temporary. It was just a costume. However, I needed to make sure. I needed to be absolutely positive. "And this," I asked, pointing at the ridiculous getup, "this is your costume for the evening?"

"Yes." He laughed. "Do I normally look like this?"

No. Definitely *not.*

"So, will you be my date? Or did I just waste fifty bucks on this rockin' plaid shirt for no reason?"

I gave myself a second to pout. My plan would have to wait. "I can throw something together, I suppose."

"You can invite your friends if you want." He walked inside and shut the door. "It is a party, after all."

I didn't really want Sloan within fifty feet of him right now, but I didn't feel like explaining that. "I could give them a call, I guess."

I grabbed my cell as I ran for the closet. Sloan answered on the first ring. "Hey, Elle. What's up?"

"Grab your red stilettos. We've got a party to attend."

I threw myself into the back of my walk-in closet, digging through boxes, and searching for one in particular. "Huh? I thought you would be…"

I stopped her. "Yeah, I did too. Look, he invited us to a party, so we're going. Be in costume and ready within the hour."

"Costume? Hell, yeah! Are you bringing the—"

"Yes." I grunted, pulling out a little red box from a stack of books. "I'm bringing the fangs."

Sloan laughed as the phone clicked off. I busted out of the closet and ran for the bathroom. Fifteen minutes later I heard a light tap on the door. "May I?" Oliver asked, walking in.

"Sure, I'm just finishing up."

I checked my hair before strutting out into my bedroom. He sat on the edge of my bed, and I watched his eyes rake down me. I knew the hoochie boots were a good idea. I took in a sharp breath. Could he look any hotter on my bed? My eyes locked on his, the absence of the buffer stinging at me, and I realized that he could in fact look so much hotter.

"I'm not complaining," he said, eyeing my legs again, "but you haven't even changed. What have you been doing in here?"

I smiled, revealing the pointed fangs now

179

securely attached to my canines.

"Oh."

I couldn't help but laugh as he immediately set upright on the bed.

I purred, running my tongue over them as I walked toward him. I sat on his lap and ran my fingers down his face. "You look so tasty. I might have to make you my snack later. You are my new favorite flavor, after all."

A low rumbling erupted from his chest as his hand tinkered around the hem of my mini skirt. "We don't get many girls like you out here on the ranch," he said, imitating his best John Wayne voice.

I whipped myself around until I was straddling his waist. "I bet you don't. How about you take me out to the barn and let's have a little fun in the hayloft?"

"Yes, ma'am." He smiled against my neck.

I started to understand Sloan's fascination. I had to admit this was kind of fun. I kissed my way down his neck, enjoying his sweet taste. I opened my mouth, allowing the fangs to graze his skin, and suddenly he gripped my ass and pulled me back. "Not yet."

I leaned up, looking him in the eye, and stuck out my lip. "But I'm thirsty."

He bit his lip and closed his eyes. "I promise you can do whatever you want to me later."

I jerked open one the buttons on his shirt. "Oh, I plan on it, cowboy."

His eyes widened as I got up. I was left to admire the full effect through his new Wranglers. "You're going to need to sex it down a bit, before we pick up Sloan," I advised, "or I won't be able to assure your safety."

"Is it a long drive?"

"No."

"Then maybe we should walk, because I'm going to need a minute after that."

I nodded and took his hand. Once outside, he leaned in closer, wrapping his arm around me as we walked. "I can't let anything happen to my naughty little vampire tonight."

"I have to admit," I said, snuggling closer, "this is a pretty exciting first date."

"Well, you are the first reason I've had to get my nose out the books since school started, so I figured I should take full advantage."

We took our time walking. I wasn't in any hurry. I finally got the chance to learn more about him. I found out he only came to Maryland due to the all expenses paid scholarship he'd earned. He had one sibling, his younger brother Dexter, who loved my X-Men poster we'd sent him for his birthday, and he had an overprotective mother who thought he was surely going to die of starvation. I made a mental note to start adding actual meals in with the sweet treats. I couldn't let my nerd function on sugar alone. He needed to get a little protein in there.

By the time we made it to Sloan's apartment, the conversation had diluted to his obsession with classic movies and my hidden passion to own my own bakeshop. I stood outside Sloan's door for a minute, trying to decide if this was a good idea or not. I was taking a hot cowboy into Sloan's house. I was surprised there weren't some kind of warning sirens going off upon his arrival on her doorstep. Oliver looked at me then at the closed door that I wasn't knocking on. "What are you waiting for?"

"Oh, nothing." I searched around for the sirens again before making three short knocks on the door.

Sloan quickly slung it open, pulling me inside. "Hey, guys, I am so excited about tonight. I love costume parties." She grabbed the little red box out of my hands. "Give me the fangs. I've got to finish my outfit."

She was about to turn around for the bathroom when she finally noticed Oliver. She stopped dead still. It was as if she'd frozen into a statue. Oliver's cheeks blushed under her stare, and I gave her a quick stab to the ribs. "Sloan." I said her name slowly and with warning in my tone. "Oliver has chosen to dress up as a cowboy tonight for his costume."

Her eyes twinkled. "I can see that."

"I'm guessing you're going as a vampire as well," he asked, eyeing the box in her hand.

She nodded. I squeezed her shoulder, trying to bring her out of the cowboy trance. I didn't want the horny to burst out when the shock faded. "I'll be right back," she said. "By the way, I invited Preston. He should be here any minute."

"That's great." I shoved her toward the bathroom then looked back at Oliver. "I'll be right back. I'm going to help Sloan with her fangs."

I pushed her in the bathroom and locked the door behind us.

"Elle." She threw her hands out in disbelief.

"What the hell were you thinking letting him come in my house looking like that?"

"I had no idea he had this planned." I laughed, because what else could I do at this point? "Imagine my surprise when he showed up on my doorstep like that."

She pointed her finger at me. "You better be glad Preston is coming with us. And hell, I still can't promise anything. Especially after a couple shots tonight."

"Just remember he is still a dorky nerd underneath. At least that's what I will be telling myself all night."

She smirked as she opened up the red box and started to apply her fangs. Soon, we were ready. We had to wait for Preston to arrive. I made sure to keep myself firmly planted between my cowboy and Sloan the entire time. She kept throwing me wicked smirks just to piss me off. I had never been happier to hear a damn doorbell ring. Sloan opened the door, and from the angle where we stood, I couldn't see Preston on the other side. Whatever his costume was had left Sloan speechless. "Oh no."

Preston's slow southern drawl echoed from the other side. "Hello, Miss Sloan. Don't you look mighty fine this evening."

She smiled, but quickly turned to me with a panicked expression on her face. I looked at her, confused, not understanding what the problem could be. Preston walked in, placing his arm around Sloan's shoulder. "Hey, y'all. Thanks for inviting us to the party."

I tried to gasp, but the air caught in my throat.

This couldn't be freaking happening. Oliver laughed next to me. "So, are you like a pale Steve Urkel?"

Preston's face brightened. "Exactly! I thought the suspenders may be a little much, but I figured, what the hell, why not?"

Why not? I bet Sloan could give a list of why nots right now. He pushed the large, awkward glasses up his nose and snapped his suspenders. "So, what do you think, Miss Elle? Can I pass as a nerd for the evening?"

Sloan glared at me. "Don't answer that."

Preston ignored her as he inspected Oliver's outfit. "Cowboy?"

Oliver nodded. "Yeah. Elle and I were talking about the movie *Young Guns* the other day, and it gave me the idea."

Preston nodded like it made perfect sense. "You wanna borrow my hat and belt buckle?"

"You have a hat?" Oliver's eyes lit up, and Sloan's face went a couple shades lighter.

"Yeah, actually, it's here. Sloan asked me to bring it over to show her the other night," he explained.

I stifled a snort and smirked at her. "I bet she did."

Preston trotted off with Oliver to retrieve what I was sure were props in Sloan's last rendezvous with Mr. Huckleberry. As soon as they left, she shook me in pure freak-out mode. "What are we going to do?"

"What do you mean?" I shrugged and looked toward the bedroom where I heard the guys talking.

"I think it's kind of funny. I mean what are the odds?"

"We have to make them switch," she pressed more seriously.

I rolled my eyes. "Come on, Sloan. They have to be the nerd and the southern gentleman every single day of their lives. Let them live a fantasy for one night. They will both go back to normal tomorrow."

She crossed her arms and pouted.

"We could always just switch for the night," I said, and it got the response I wanted.

She slapped me. "Stay away from my cowboy."

"Well, I can't promise anything after a couple shots."

She shot daggers at me when the boys came back in the room. Oliver was now adorned in a cowboy hat and a large gold belt buckle. Sloan whimpered next to me. This was just going to be too much tonight. "Everyone ready?" Oliver asked, opening the front door.

"Oh, yeah," I said, walking past Preston. "I am so ready for this."

Just because I couldn't help myself, I snapped one of Preston's suspenders as I went by. "I'm thinking body shots tonight." I winked at him, revealing my fangs.

If you were quiet enough, I would have sworn you could hear Sloan's head explode behind me. Just to be safe, I ran and engulfed myself in Oliver's arms. "What do you say, cowboy? Body shots?"

"I told you I'm yours for the taking tonight, oh, evil temptress of the night."

"Hmm…you shouldn't have said that."

I pulled him out the door and we started walking down the street toward our party. Sloan even lightened up enough to start skipping as we rounded the corner. Two vampires, a cowboy, and a nerd. I could hear the *Twilight Zone* theme song echoing in my head. This was going to be one hell of a night.

Chapter Eighteen

SHOTS

Rowdy Randy's Pub had a giant banner hanging out front announcing the costume party and half priced shots. College kids were coming out of the woodwork. A bouncer stood at the door, letting people in as others came out. Music blasted out of the open windows. I worried the tired looking brick building might start to crumble from the deep beat of the bass that rattled the glass.

The bouncer took one look at Sloan and recognized her. He waved us forward, bypassing the long line. Good thing she and Ava were regulars on Friday night. "Thanks, Gus." Sloan smiled at the abnormally tall guy, and he nodded without saying a word.

I slipped around the black rope that blocked the doorway and pulled Oliver along with me. We waded through the crowd and found an open spot at the bar. A very small open spot. We squeezed in tight together as Sloan waved down the bartender.

Oliver's lips pressed against my ear. "I had no idea it would be this crowded," he said above the buzz of the chatter around us.

I wrapped my arm around his waist. "It's not a problem."

I inched even closer to him, our hips connecting, and he got my point. His arm slung around my shoulder, allowing my lips to come mere inches from his chin. I leaned even further into him and he grinned down at me. "Definitely not a problem."

Sloan handed shots over her shoulder to Preston, and he passed them out to each of us. Once everyone had two each, she turned around and held hers up. "So the game is called I've Never," she explained, twirling the shot of something blue around in her fingers. "I'm guessing everyone knows the rules."

"Yes." I rolled my eyes. Everyone knew the rules of that game. "If you have done it, you take a shot."

Oliver eyed his muddy brown shots cautiously. "Umm, don't you think we should maybe ease into this? I mean, hardcore shots right off the bat might not be the best idea for the longevity of our night."

"Pony up, cowboy." Sloan smirked and dinged her shot glass against his. "Or is that belt buckle all you're packing?"

His eyes narrowed at her. "I am more concerned with Elle and yourself," he said, pointing at our shots. "I can handle it."

"We'll see about that." She grinned and held up her first shot. "I've done a lot of things, but I've never watched porn on my phone during class."

Without moving their heads, the guys shot a glance toward each other, but neither of them raised their shot glasses. Pussies. I picked up my glass and took my shot.

Oliver's eyes widened. "Eloise?"

I shrugged. "It was an accident. Ava stole my phone and left me some very vile surprises."

Preston sniggered and took his shot. "Same thing happened to me. At least that's the story I'm going with." Preston slammed his empty glass against the bar behind him. "And might I say, Elle. You took that shot like a champ. Do you mind if I call you Elle?"

"Tonight? Tonight you can call me anything you want," I said, winking at him.

Sloan kicked me under the bar. "So, you taking the shot or not cowboy?" I asked, looking down at Oliver's glass.

He sighed and shrugged. "I've never watched porn in class."

"Nerd," Preston said, pushing his glasses up his nose.

Oliver snorted, motioning for the bartender to send Preston and me another round. "My turn," Preston announced. "I've done a lot of things, but I have never kissed anyone of the same sex."

They both stared at us. They stared at us with evil grins. Sloan and I glanced at each other. Neither of us took a shot.

"Come on," Preston pouted, "you could at least lie to me."

"She's not my type," we both stated at the same time.

Sloan looked over at Oliver, and he quickly glanced down at his glass. "What?"

"Your turn."

Oliver took a deep breath. "I've done a lot of things, but I have never spied on my best friend in the library."

Sloan's nose wrinkled up, but she took her shot. It was my turn. I was determined to get alcohol in that boy's system. I wracked my brain, trying to figure out something I could say that would force Oliver to take a shot. It was times like these that made me wish I was more innocent. Then again, if I was that innocent, I probably wouldn't be trying to get my date drunk. Sloan could tell I was thinking hard, and I noticed she started doing some crude gestures toward her mouth. Then it finally hit me what she was trying to convey.

"I have done a lot of things, but I've never received oral sex in a public place."

Preston quickly downed his shot. "A broom closet counts, right?"

Sloan gave him a quick nod before she downed her own, and I patiently waited for Oliver. He raised the glass to his lips and smiled at me. "Tonight will be the last time you'll get to use that one on me."

He took his shot to a round of howls from the rest of us. The party was officially starting. Thirty minutes and a handful of shots later, we had moved our party over to a booth in the corner. The game had changed.

Preston held out his glass, prepared to make his latest wager. "Bet you girls two shots slutty Ghostbuster over there has on a thong."

"I'll take that bet." I took a long look at Ghostbuster girl. "I bet she's commando."

"How the hell do you two think we are even going to find that out?" Oliver asked, just about the time the drunk girl bent over, flashing a full view of her naked ass.

"Damn it." Preston slammed his glass on the table. "How could you tell?"

I shrugged. "If you can slut up the Ghostbusters, you are just that kind of girl."

"Take your shots." Sloan eagerly leaned over and nudged Oliver as well.

Oliver sat back. "What? I didn't bet anything."

"Preston is officially representing the males in this game."

I wholeheartedly agreed, and he took his double round out of fear of getting called a pussy again. You had to love the male ego. I stood and realized I had hit that spot. That grand little spot in my alcohol tolerance level that was right between sauced and take me home, honey. Sloan realized it too. "Oh, Willis Richard Fitzwright, how I have missed you. And it's not even a holiday!"

The boys looked utterly confused. "Will His Dick Fit Right is my drunk name," I explained. "At least, that's what Sloan calls me."

Preston turned back and forth between us. "You two are the weirdest girls I have ever met."

"Willis," Sloan screamed, standing, "I think it's time we showed these boys how to have a good time."

"Wait a second." I set my glass down and turned toward her. "What level of a good time are we talking about here?"

Sloan went into deep concentration as she looked down and inspected the boys. "Under current circumstances, I would suggest level four, at least until we get the cowboy a little more drunk."

"My cowboy or your cowboy?"

She grinned. "All the cowboys."

"Works for me." I grabbed Oliver's hand, pulling him up as Sloan repeated the gesture on Preston.

We dragged them toward the bar. I looked over at Sloan. "What's the order for tonight?"

"Do you even have to ask?" She shoved Preston against the bar. "Body shots."

Preston's eyes lit up, and he immediately jumped up on the bar. Oliver was more hesitant, so I gave him an encouraging slap on the ass. Okay, so it was more for my benefit than his, but it still got the point across, and he obeyed. I crawled up on a stool and started ripping buttons open. "Should I leave the suspenders?" Sloan asked, snapping one of them.

"Please?"

"Then you don't touch the hat."

I ran my hand down Oliver's now bare chest and smiled. "I could care less about the hat right now."

I handed Oliver the bottle before placing my head at his stomach, looking up at him. He realized his cue and poured the shot down his chest. I let my fangs scratch against his chest before letting my tongue slip out, licking up my shot. The shot burned my throat, but Oliver tasted too damn good to stop. I was about to sink my teeth in for a real taste when I heard a high-pitched shrill from behind me. "What the heck is this? I know you two are kinky, but damn."

I shot a look over my shoulder to find Ava standing behind us with her eyebrows raised, glancing between my half naked cowboy and the nerd that was currently getting violated by Sloan. I turned and gave her a fang-filled smile, which she returned.

"I got your message." She winked at us. "How could I possibly resist a costume party?"

Her own fangs burst out through her smile. That was when I noticed Brad standing behind her dressed like a lumberjack. A lumberjack with about eight fang sized hickeys on his neck. I rolled my eyes. She had the nerve to call me kinky. I pointed at the empty spot next to Oliver on the bar. "Want to join the fun? I think we could fit a lumberjack up here."

Oliver jumped off the bar. "I don't think so." He grabbed me around my waist. "Your turn is over."

He swung me around, flashing me a smile before he dropped to his knees. I felt the cool liquid begin to drip down my leg as he poured out the shot. His tongue pressed hot against my inner thigh as I grabbed onto the bar for support. It instantly started moving up, sparking electricity into every part of me. He kept going, even after he surpassed the spot where he had started the shot. His tongue flicked teasingly along the edge of my panty line as his hand slipped up the back of my skirt. I grabbed a fistful of silky hair, jerking his head back so I could look down at his face. "That's it." The ripple of ecstasy continued down my spine. "Change clothes

193

with Preston right now."

He looked up at me, confused, and I turned to Preston. "You two need to change clothes *right now*."

Preston laughed, but then his expression fell. "You're serious?"

"Yes," Sloan and I stated at the same time.

Oliver stood, encircling me in his arms, smirking down at me. "We can't change clothes in the middle of a bar."

I scooted him over closer to Preston. "Yes, you can. And you will."

Worried looks ran across both their faces as I heard Brad chuckle behind them. "I would suggest you do whatever the hell they want," he said, gesturing toward the marks on his neck. "Trust me, you don't want to disobey a vampire."

Oliver glanced down at me, waiting for me to say something, hoping for me to let him off the hook. "Strip it. Pants and all."

Preston eagerly started unhooking his suspenders as Sloan worked on his jeans. "We are really doing this?"

I ignored him, jerking off his shirt. I threw it over to Sloan, who threw me back a white button up with red and yellow stripped suspenders. My mouth watered as I watched Oliver unbutton his jeans. The exchange was quick and hardly anyone in the bar noticed. There was only one thing left. I pulled the hat off Oliver's head and trotted over to Preston. I smiled brilliantly at him before coveting his glasses and handing over his hat. "You were cute while it lasted."

"Thanks, Miss Elle."

Sloan growled over his shoulder.

I couldn't tell whether it was due to the fact that I told Preston he was cute, or the fact that Preston had put on the cowboy hat. Probably a little of both. I quickly returned to Oliver, placing the glasses delicately on his face.

He smirked at me. "Better now?"

"Much."

I wrapped my fingers around one of his suspenders and pulled. "Well, it's been fun," I shouted over my shoulder as I dragged him through the crowd.

He wrapped his arms around my waist and whispered in my ear. "Where are we going, oh, evil mistress of the night?"

"Somewhere dark and abandoned."

My feet lifted off the ground. Oliver slung my legs around his waist as he carried me more swiftly through the crowd. "Then what?"

I giggled innocently, placing my face between his neck and shoulder. I let my tongue graze across the skin. "I told you that you were my new favorite flavor."

I sunk my teeth in, fangs and all. He grunted loudly, gripping his fingers across my ass as we busted through the back door of the bar into the alley. I lapped my tongue over the bruised skin, hoping to sooth the pain. "Mmm...tasty Oliver."

Chapter Nineteen

MERRY

The brick scraped my back, but the unpleasant sensation was easily drowned out by every other Oliver-induced sensation. I twitched every time the rim of his glasses scraped against my skin. I desperately tried to lower myself, making his tongue rise faster, but he held me firmly in place against the wall. I balled my fingers in his hair, tugging just hard enough for him to get the point. The point being that teasing me like this was going to land him on his back, ready to learn this vampire sought something more risqué than a little blood.

His breath ran up my leg. "Patience."

I panted harder, unconcerned that someone could walk out the back door and find us in the alley at any second. His fingers began to trace the line of his tongue until they reached the corner of my panty line. I whined when he stopped. His teeth grazed up my leg, taking small bites every few seconds.

"Oliver."

196

My head fell back against the wall as I desperately tried to hold it together. My legs started trembling as my fingers tightened in his hair. I clenched my eyes trying to concentrate on something else so I managed to keep the sensation without throwing myself over the edge.

I repeated nursery rhymes in my head.

"Little Bo Peep has lost her sheep..." this was not going to work, "and she doesn't know where to find them."

Little Bo Beep wasn't going to suffice. I had to admit it. I was Little Miss Muffet sitting on her nerd tuffet while he ate her curds and whey.

"Oliver—"

His free hand snaked around my back, pulling me down to him. I was gone. My knees buckled as the muscles in my stomach ignited. I wanted to collapse on top of him, but he held me firmly in place.

He slowed his rhythm as he began to hum a contented chorus. I released my hold on him as I panted. He placed a chaste kiss on the inside of my thigh. "So, that's how you tame a vampire?"

I wanted to scowl, but I felt too damn good. "Tame me?" I laughed, pulling him to face me. "You just unleashed me."

His eyes almost seemed to sparkle behind his glasses. I grabbed hold of one of his suspenders and pulled. "Come on, I'm in need a flat surface."

He eagerly followed me down the alley until we came to the street. "That's flat." He pointed to a hood of a car on the side of the street.

"Umm, not quite what I'm looking for."

197

We continued to walk. Well I continued to walk and pull his ass along with me. "That's flat," he suggested again, now pointing to bench sitting in front of the bus stop sign.

"Patience." I tugged him along faster.

He didn't realize, but I already had a specific flat surface in mind, and it was only a half block away. He moaned behind me as we trudged on. "You know, it's kind of difficult to walk in this condition."

I sniggered. I pulled him up to my back, letting my hand run over the source of his tortuous condition. His hands gripped my thighs as he shoved himself up against my ass. I pushed him away. "No humping the vampire, or she might get overly excited and bite somewhere she has been forbidden to."

I gave him another sensual rub before bolting up the street. He raced after me. The trees started to get slightly thicker and I knew we were close. Sure enough, just in front of us to left was the desired flat surface I had been in search of.

We were at the Grove City Park. The trees were thick, and it was completely abandoned. I dragged him closer. He glanced around anxiously. "Where are we going?"

I stopped dead still, smiling to myself. I raised my hand and pointed into the distance. "Now that's what you call a flat surface."

He squinted into the darkness, trying to make out what stood in front of us. He glanced down at me, raising a questioning eye. "A merry-go-round?"

I smiled. "Why do you think they call it a merry-go-round?" I snapped his suspender and grinned when it popped.

"So you *are* a kinky mistress of the night."

I maneuvered him into the right spot before pushing him back. He fell with a slight bang against the metal. I worried that I might have been too rough, but he just grinned up at me.

The cool sting of the metal hissed against my skin as I climbed over him. I gave one tiny push with my left foot, sending us spinning for the hell of it. It only made sense to go around while we got our merry on. I crawled up and straddled him, playing with the buttons along his shirt. I officially had my prey in sight, and now it was time for the kill. I slid the suspenders off his shoulders as I bent down to run kisses and light bites along his neck.

His hand ran up the back of my skirt, gripping me tightly. He moaned, pulling me forward. "Who is teasing now?"

I halted my attack long enough to start relieving him of unnecessary garments. As it turned out, it was all pretty unnecessary. I slid his shirt open, only to be distracted by the firm lines of his chest. I itched to taste every single inch of him. My lips caught the edge of his stomach as my fingers played with the buttons of his jeans.

I was about to let my hand take the plunge when he flipped me over. My back fell against the cool metal. "I don't think so, vampy." He laughed against my ear. "The nerd teaches the lessons."

I licked across my fangs as I arched myself up into him. He pushed his glasses up his nose before flinging himself on top of me. His body ground

199

against my own as he desperately sought to push my skirt higher up my legs. I busied myself with his neck while he prepared. I was determined to follow his lead. Even kinky mistresses of the night could be good little students.

He pulled back, hovering over me, and I reflexively scooted myself down into position. He ran his hand lightly over my thigh, squeezing it gently. I placed my hands around his lower back and held on. He entered me slowly, running his nose across my cheek. I didn't realize he was holding his breath until he moaned through gritted teeth. I pulled up against him, needing more.

He held his balance with his right arm as he gripped the other around my backside. He started out slowly, moving in a smooth, steady rhythm as he hissed out his pleasure. When my fingers dug into his back, he started picking up the pace. My hips moved in tandem with his, lusting for that deep connection every time he pulled away.

I leaned my head back so I could look up at his face. I wanted to watch his eyes close in pleasure behind his glasses. I wanted to watch them inch down his nose as the force with which he entered jarred them out of place. Most importantly, I wanted to push them back up his nose and watch him smile at the gesture.

I knew he was getting close when he buried his face in my shoulder. It was a sure sign he was trying to hold on. I knew that feeling. I loved that feeling. I loved stumbling along that edge between anticipation and ecstasy. I could feel myself approaching the cliff. He grabbed one of my legs, pulling it up and over his shoulder. I squealed at the new sense of pleasure the slight change in position caused. My hands gripped his shoulder and ran up to his hair.

He was encouraged by the sense of urgency I portrayed. "Let me see your fangs."

I smiled as the pleasure ripped through me. "Oliver."

I squeaked, clenching onto him for support as I fell over the edge for the second time tonight.

He soon followed me, letting my legs go, falling gently onto my stomach. His heartbeat thrummed wildly against my chest. He placed subtle, tired kisses along my collarbone. We lay there for a few minutes, too consumed by our own glorious fortune to move. I felt him smile against my skin. "What?" I breathed deeply, running my fingers along his bare skin.

"Sloan is going to bring this up every time we play that stupid game now."

"True, but you have my permission to shoot back with a bathroom stall at the pirate museum."

He raised his head to look at me. "Pirate museum?"

"It was a Johnny Depp thing...don't ask."

He shook his head and placed his cheek back against my chest. I closed my eyes, enjoying every last second. I felt a vibration against my shoulder. I tilted my head up and listened harder to realize Oliver hummed the Imperial March as he twisted a string of my hair around his finger. I giggled and flicked the edge of his glasses. "What?" He glanced up. "Too nerdy for you?"

"No." I smiled, rubbing his cheek. "Just nerdy enough."

Chapter Twenty

MORNING

Someone should warn you that waking up with your bare ass against metal might not be the most pleasant experience. In all honesty, it stung like hell, and I fretted it might be frostbitten, which I was sure wouldn't be very attractive. I sat up on my elbows, spitting hair out of my mouth, quickly realizing I was still wearing my fangs. I groaned. It was hard to enjoy the excesses of your night out on the town when you woke with sunlight beaming down in your eyes. That was one fact vampires got right.

I felt certain my mood was deteriorating until I looked further down my naked body that lay across the merry-go-round. At first glance, it looked as if I had four legs and an extra set of arms coming out of my waist, but upon further focused inspection, it became clear the extra appendages belonged to an extremely hung over, yet unbearably adorable nerd. Oliver's face was snuggled on my stomach, his glasses awry on his face, leading down to his glorious little ass that bounced sunlight off it like a crystal.

I chuckled to myself. It would be a good morning after all, it seemed. I took the opportunity and ran my fingers through his tousled locks, which caused him to smile in his sleep. I smiled brilliantly in return. My stomach decided it was too impatient to wait for me and rumbled loudly into Oliver's ear, causing him to stir. He grunted, shifting his face around on my stomach, as his eyes fluttered open. He winced as soon as the light invaded, and his grunt turned into an outright moan of agony.

I laughed, allowing my hand to run down to the back of his neck. "Good morning to you too, sunshine."

He looked up at me from under his messy hair and grinned sheepishly. "Who let that damn thing out of its cage?" he asked, throwing the sun a scowling look.

"Beats me." I shrugged. "But it's probably a warning. Even though this ancient park has been abandoned, people still use the running trails. Joggers may start arriving soon."

Oliver slowly sat up until he looked into my eyes. "Are you trying to say that having sex on a playground isn't appropriate in the daytime?" A small smirk developed on his lips.

"Not me," I assured him. "But other people, less adventurous people, would disagree with me."

"Oh." He laughed.

"Unfortunately for us, some of those people carry badges that allow them to put handcuffs on us

204

and charge us with silly crimes like public indecency."

His mouth dropped open in mock horror. "The bastards!"

I nodded in agreement. "The way of the daylight world."

He scoffed loudly, rolling over. "Then I much prefer the night. May I roam the dark abyss of the midnight realm with you?"

My lips smoothed into a line as I pretended to think it over. "I'll think about it." I tapped my finger on my chin. "However, I'd be much more inclined to agree if I wasn't so hungry."

His eyes narrowed as his hand traced down his neck over the dark bruises I'd left. "You mean I wasn't enough to satisfy you?"

"You were just a snack." I licked my lips enticingly. "But if you want, I'll make a meal out of you later."

He chuckled darkly as he sat up. "I'll remember that."

So would I.

He stood, reaching out his hand to me. I took it, allowing him to help me up. I stood there watching in a daze as he fumbled around gathering up our clothes. He threw me an odd look as he handed me my panties. "What?"

"I like you." It came out like a confession rather than a fact.

His smile grew as he slipped his boxers up over his hips. "I hope. Or I just pulled out all my best moves for nothing."

I rolled my eyes while I put on my own clothes.

"I'm being serious."

One moment he was buttoning his jeans, and the next I found him lifting me up in the air, wrapping my bare legs around his waist. "I know." He smiled, pulling my face down to kiss my lips. "I like you too."

I smiled against his lips. He gave me an affectionate squeeze across my backside. "I don't sing *Star Wars* to just anybody, you know?"

"That's probably a good idea." I chuckled, eliciting a playful smack on my ass.

Before our playtime could go further, because that was where my lips were persuading us to go, my stomach roared again. He kissed my cheek, setting me back down on the ground. "Come on, let's find you a more fulfilling snack."

We dressed and exited the empty playground without notice. We headed back to Oliver's apartment because it was closer than mine. Luckily, only a few people witnessed our walk of shame. A little old lady walking her tiny, yet extremely furry dog gave us a disgusted "humph" as we walked past, but quickly changed her tune when I flashed her a fang-filled smile. A few blocks later, a random frat boy gave Oliver an awkward high five as he passed. The most humorous and memorable of encounters came when we rounded a corner, only to run head first into Sloan and Preston. We each stumbled backward, apologizing profusely before we realized who we'd run into.

"Elle?" Sloan asked with eyes opened wide.

"Sloan?"

Sloan wore nothing but a long sleeved flannel

shirt and a large ten-gallon hat. Preston was, of course, shirtless, left only with his jeans and an extra-large belt buckle. We studied each other for a moment, taking it all in. "Where are your clothes?" I finally managed to ask.

"Where's your dignity?" She laughed, poking a finger into my crazed hair.

I shot her a look, pointing at her pant-less figure, daring her to start comparing dignity with me. She scratched her head underneath the oversized hat. "I don't know." She glanced down at herself. "Where my clothes are, I mean. We were actually in the act of backtracking in hopes of figuring that one out."

"I think I remember taking your bra off while we were still at the bar," Preston said sleepily. "Or maybe it was your pantyhose."

I shook my head, grinning at her. "Nice one, Sloan. I mean, losing your clothes? I thought that only happened to Ava on Margarita Mondays."

She gave me a short scowl. "You look wonderful, by the way. Is that dirt on your face?"

She had me there, although the merry-go-round was cleaner than you would think, or at least it used to be. "Do you need help finding your clothes?"

She sighed loudly for her own benefit, because it prompted Preston to pull her into his side. "No. I think it's a lost cause. Anything I lost at that bar, I don't really want back."

"True. Some lonely geek probably stole your panties."

"Ugh." She groaned. "Thank you for that image."

Right after, Oliver added a very offended.

"Hey!"

I turned to him, kissing his shoulder. "You're a nerd, sweetie, not a geek. There is a difference."

"There is?" Sloan asked, but quickly changed it to a statement. "I mean, there is!"

I threw her a dirty look as Oliver frowned. Luckily, Preston intervened. "Dude. I'm pretty sure geeks don't leave the bar with their fingers halfway up a vampire's skirt. You're safe."

Oliver gave himself a very self-reassuring nod, and I tried not to smile. The boys gave each other sleepy goodbyes, promising to hang out again in the near future, as Sloan gave me a quick hug. "I expect a full report by noon tomorrow."

I gave her a silent salute as we continued our walk home. Oliver's apartment complex made me drool. I'd been there several times now, and it still left me awe. The place was fully furnished, especially when compared to my place, where I considered a couple Johnny Depp posters extravagant artwork. Oliver led me straight to the kitchen, pulling out a chair at the table while Scuba affectionately tried to maneuver his very large body into the chair with me.

Oliver started going through the cabinets, and suddenly Scuba was less interested in me and more interested in his bowl. "I don't have that many options," he explained sadly, opening random cabinets, only to find them empty. He filled Scuba's bowl with food before going to check the last cabinet next to the fridge. "I don't suppose you're a fan of Cap'n Crunch?"

"The Captain?" I smiled. "We go way back. Care

to fix me a bowl while I remove my fangs?"

He smiled, relieved, as he retrieved milk from the fridge. "Sure. There is a bathroom right around the corner."

I scurried off into the bathroom because I'd been unwilling to tell him how badly I needed to pee. After accomplishing all the necessities, including the removal of my fangs, I took the time to look at myself in the mirror. Sloan had been right. My hair was horrendous. It literally stuck out in every direction, and the back was wadded up in knots. I looked like Medusa, except my snakes were on crack. I tried to comb my fingers through it, but it was impossible to tame. I eventually gave up and returned to the kitchen. I tried to remind myself he hadn't run away screaming yet, so maybe that was a good sign, or maybe his glasses weren't as strong as I thought.

We were both relatively quiet as we devoured our breakfast. We did manage to throw in a few mouth-full laughs at each other, especially after he caught me trying comb my hair again.

"Don't hurt yourself." He laughed, between bites. "You can use my shower if you want. That looks like it could use some conditioner."

It was always reassuring when a boy referred to your hair as "that" because he was too afraid to call it by its proper name. I stuck my tongue out at him. "Not everyone can be blessed with such perfectly manageable hair as you. Even now, messy and knotted, your hair looks sexy. It's not fair."

He snorted into his spoon. "That's your opinion. Personally, I think yours looks rather distinguishing."

"Distinguishing?" I sipped the last of my milk out of the bowl. "Thanks a lot. That's just a nice way of saying you're uniquely ugly in a way I've never seen before."

He rolled his eyes as he took our bowls to the sink. "Yep. That's exactly why all I want to do is pull you into my bed and snuggle all day."

"You're an odd one, Edwards."

"Back at ya, Duncan."

He pulled me into his side, kissing the top of my tangled head. Oliver took Scuba outside then we both took showers in separate bathrooms, despite my willingness to a share a shower with him. I thought he knew we were both too tired at the moment to handle any more strenuous activities. He sweetly offered me a pair of his pajama pants and an oversized t-shirt. When I walked into his bedroom, I found him lying in his bed already snuggled up next to a pillow, wearing only his boxers and glasses. I reflexively bit my lip.

Rest, I told myself, I needed rest first. I stepped over Scuba, who now had a very large bone to chew on, and slowly crawled onto the bed and replaced the pillow with myself. He instantly moved closer to me. "I've been waiting for you."

His hair was still wet, and it felt cool against my flushed skin. "Sorry." I already felt the urge to close my heavy eyes. "The hot water felt so nice."

"I know." He yawned. "It makes you sleepy."

I hummed my agreement. Our breaths slowed, and I felt myself sinking deeper into him.

***

I awoke a little after three o'clock. Oliver was still asleep, having rolled over onto his stomach. I lay there staring out at his room, thinking as I noticed the large flat screen TV for the first time. I sat up, cocking my head as I examined it. "Elle?" His voice still sounded groggy as his finger tapped my side.

I looked innocently over at him.

"What are you thinking so hard about?" He rolled over so he could see me better.

I looked at the TV and then back to him. "I realized I still have questions about you."

The happiness in his face faded as he propped himself up on his elbow. "I've been moving too fast, haven't I?" He sighed before adding, "Shit."

"No. I didn't mean it like that, and if I did, it wouldn't be your fault. I attacked you on top of a library desk, for heaven's sake. It's just, I still have things I want to know about you."

"Okay." He sat up next to me, continuing to rub his hand over my leg. "Ask me anything."

I shot a quick glance back at the TV and figured, what the hell? "Are you rich?"

He stared at me a moment before busting out into laughter. "I guess it looks that way, doesn't it?" He ran his fingers through his hair. "No, Elle. I am definitely not rich."

My eyes narrowed in thought. "But..."

He held up his hand. "This isn't my condo. It belongs to my aunt. She owns the entire complex. She agreed to let me live here free of charge as long

211

as I was continuing my education. As soon as I graduate, I'm back out on the streets."

It was silent for a moment as I took in his words. "So, you're a poor college kid too?"

His smile grew. "With a very generous aunt."

I didn't know why, but I felt mildly relieved. It made us even again. He continued to look over at me expectantly. "Anything else?"

I smiled as I wiped the sleep out of my eyes. "Yes. I want to know everything."

He sighed, pushing his glasses back up his nose. "You sure?"

I ran my finger down the rim, biting my lip. "I'm positive."

He gave me a resigned grunt as he scooted back against his pillow, adjusting himself into a comfortable position. "Okay, but remember, you already had sex with me. You can't take it back."

I rolled my eyes dramatically, crawling over to straddle his waist. "Just give it to me straight. I want to know."

"Well," he began, pulling me up closer, "I may or may not own a pair of Power Ranger pajamas."

I opened my mouth to speak, but he beat me to the punch. "Not the pink one," he said quickly, predicting my question. "It's the green one. He's much more manly."

"Of course." I tried to stifle my giggle. "Please continue."

He grinned up at me, laughing. "Did I mention I can't cook? I almost burned my house down trying to make a Pop Tart once."

"But you baked me cookies."

"I brought you cookies," he said, shooting me a shy smile. "You assumed I baked them."

My mouth gaped. "You got me fake cookies?"

"Fake? They weren't fake. They were eatable." He tried to look offended and apologetic all at the same time.

"What else?" I demanded seriously, but I kept giggling as I tried to scold him.

He immediately started shaking his head. "Not yet." He grinned triumphantly. "Now it's your turn."

I frowned, having expected it wouldn't be that easy. "Remember," I said, smiling at him, "you already bribed me with fake cookies. You can't take them back."

He snorted, tickling my sides, and I fell over in a fit of laughter. I knew from the very moment I laid on eyes on Oliver Edwards that the sex would be amazing, but I was pleasantly surprised to find out that everything else about him was just as good. He hovered over me with his dazzling eyes, glistening down at me, and I felt an overwhelming happiness build inside of me. "Spill it, missy."

I settled back against his pillow, deciding which embarrassing life fact I wanted to start with, and decided upon the one prudent to this conversation. I looked him dead in the eye, keeping my face utterly serious. "I've watched *Return of the Jedi* thirty-six times."

He stared at me a second, his eyes narrowing, and then without notice, he busted out in a round of laughter. "You're a nerd. I knew it!"

I couldn't deny it, and I wouldn't, anyway. We

both continued to laugh as he rolled over on top of me, showering me with kisses.

Chapter Twenty-One

WARNING SIGNS

Oliver and I became an inseparable pair. We switched roles effortlessly between our tutor and student relationship, baker and customer, and my personal favorite, boyfriend and girlfriend.

Yes. Oliver Edwards was my boyfriend.

It was official.

We confirmed it on social media and everything.

We continued our daily tutoring sessions at *our* spot in the library. He expanded my coffee knowledge by allowing me to sample his every day, and I always sneaked him a cupcake when he wasn't looking, for old times' sake. Sometimes we even made a detour to the poetry section, even though the secret spot wasn't required for us to be alone. We always went to Oliver's apartment when we wanted privacy.

Oliver's couch was the ideal make-out place. It was made of some kind of special Italian leather. I could sit on that couch and kiss Oliver for ages. We always went to my place for dinner, though. Oliver barely had plates, let alone pots and pans.

He stood behind me, his nose stuck in the air, appreciatively sniffing toward the pot I pulled off the stove. His hair was still wet from the shower he'd taken. He'd been in the laboratory all day perfecting some kind of sciency cocktail for his latest project. He said he needed to wash the chemical smell off.

I figured if Oliver wanted to get naked in my bathroom, so be it.

He inched closer to the bubbling pot. "What is that?"

I held up the pot of steaming liquid, moving it to a cold burner. "Soup."

"Yes. I can see that. What kind? It smells divine."

"You think everything I cook smells divine."

"What can I say? I'm honest to a fault." He peeked into the pot. "It smells like tomatoes. Does it have tomatoes?"

I smirked at him. "Possibly."

We sat on the couch next to each other, our giant bowls of soup in our laps. He wiggled down deep into his usual spot, his face lit up with anticipation. "Ready to finish our *Superman* marathon?"

I grabbed the remote off the coffee table and threw it at him. "How can I deny you when you smile at me like that? Plus, I could never turn down a date with Clark Kent."

Unless my other option was a date with Oliver Edwards. I'd choose Oliver every time. Sometimes I wondered if maybe he had a superhero alter ego as well, and he managed to hide it from me every day. We finished dinner, and Oliver reached over to take my bowl. "You don't have to do the dishes," I told him for the third time this week.

"You cook and I clean. It's how our relationship works."

I snuggled into my pillow, prepared to enjoy the sight of Oliver doing dishes in my kitchen. My cell phone beeped next to me, and I scooted up to grab it off the coffee table. A text caught my eye.

Dad: *Why haven't you returned my calls? Who are you spending your time with that you can't return a phone call. And your midterm grades haven't arrived. Email them to me tonight.*

I threw the phone away from me the same time it marked the message as read. "Shit. When did he learn how to text?"

Oliver turned off the water at the sink. "Who?"

I stared at the phone that now lay on my floor. I waited for it to catch fire like hell had somehow found me. Oliver walked back into the living room. "Elle, are you all right?"

"Yeah." I very cautiously picked the phone back up and deleted the text. "I just wasn't expecting my dad to text me. He's never done that before."

I'd ignored his calls and voicemails. I guessed stooping to text was next on his list. "You don't exactly look thrilled to hear from your dad."

217

I carefully set the phone back on the coffee table, on the farthest corner from where I sat. "He's a tad overbearing."

"About what?"

"Everything."

I answered it too quickly. It immediately threw up a red flag. Oliver came over and sat beside me. "Elle, you look like you're about to cry."

His hand touched my shoulder, and I had to fight back the tears. I didn't want Oliver to know about Bartholomew. My father would hate him. He'd find something unsatisfactory about him, and then, slowly but surely, create a wedge between us.

"It's nothing. He just wants to see my midterm grades."

"Ah. And you don't want him to see your anatomy grade."

"Pretty much."

My hand shook. I clutched it around my knee to keep it still. "You're already bringing it up. You can show him your final grade. If you keep up your pace, you should easily get a B."

I nodded, hoping he didn't see the tears well up. That wouldn't be good enough for my dad. "Do you mind if we put a hold on the movie marathon? I should probably finish up those study questions so I can focus on my quiz for this week tomorrow."

"Yeah, sure. We can study."

I bit my lip. Oliver adjusted his glasses.

It hurt to say it. "I should probably study alone tonight."

I reached up and pulled the hem of his shirt down over the edge of his pants to cover up the skin that peeked out. "I tend to get distracted when you're here. At the library, I can convince myself I can't seduce you with so many witnesses, but here…"

"What if I studied in the other room?"

I patted him softly on the leg. "I'm glad you think so highly of my self-control, but yeah…that won't work."

He pursed his lips. "You're kicking me out?"

"Don't say it like that."

He leaned over and kissed my cheek. "I understand. I want you to do well too."

I pulled him into a hug. "Thank you."

I wanted nothing more than to somehow pull the impossible and stay here with him next year, whether it was because my father finally became a real live human who could accept faults in people, or I finally accepted the fact that I'm meant to be parentless. Oliver gathered up his things, and I set a container of extra soup on top of his stack of books in his arms. "I made extra in case you needed a snack later, or breakfast tomorrow."

He leaned over his books to kiss me. "You're an angel."

As he closed the door behind him, I collapsed against it. And I cried.

I always had this constant sensation that I would eventually lose everything good in my life. Or more accurately, it would be snatched away from me.

Back on the sideline. Back to being forced to enjoy the pleasantries of my fantasy worlds as opposed to the beautiful reality of life with Oliver.

Chapter Twenty-Two

DEAD WEEK

Dead week. It was that awkward seven days between the last day of your classes and when final exams started. Everyone was in the library. Oliver and I had our usual table in the back. Sloan and Preston took the one to our left, while Ava and Brad held down the couch and small table behind us. We all had our to-do lists and worked in relative silence. It was go-time. Anatomy would be my very last final the following week, which meant I had five other exams to study for and take before I had to focus on that test, which loomed over me like a giant anvil of doom.

Gretchen and I provided the group with study time snacks. Oliver pulled off his sweater while enjoying one of my new blueberry delight cupcakes. I had a giant double fudge brownie next to my book. Oliver glanced over at me and noticed me staring. He wiped the blue icing from his lips. "Eyes on your book."

I sat my chin in my palm. "Some things are worth failing for."

He rolled his eyes. "Summer break," he said confidently. "We just have to make it until summer break."

The thought caused my heart to ache. Oliver had this grand plan to travel this summer. He wanted to take me to DC to see the capital and visit the museums because I'd never been. He already had an itinerary planned out for us. I wanted to take him up on his offer. I could see it in my mind. We'd sit together on the steps of the Lincoln Memorial, looking out over the mall, watching the sun set behind the Washington Monument while he rattled on about the history and the logistics of it all. I would listen quietly, taking in his every word and the sound of his voice. We'd eat dinner in Chinatown amid the bright lights and noise of the tourist crowds, and then we would retreat to our hotel, riding the metro to the outskirts of the city.

I *needed* that daydream to come true.

I needed this lock on my heart to be broken and the barrier between me and my own dreams to be torn down. I wanted to live life outside my father's rules without the fear of the heartbreak my mother caused me. I wanted a fresh start. A new blank page to start a new chapter of my life. No backstory. No old burdens to dampen the new scenes.

A balled-up piece of paper hit me on the side of my face. I whipped around to see a smug Sloan smiling in my direction. "Study," she mouthed, shooting me a very motherly type stare.

I stuck my tongue out at her and diverted my attention back to my work. Oliver's chair scooted in my direction, the wood of the seat knocking against mine. He didn't look at me, he simply moved his books over so he could reach them. Our ankles locked together beneath the table, and he smiled as he continued to read his book.

I smiled too—I couldn't stop it.

I didn't think I understood what actual happiness meant until now, until I experienced that small moment in which life, even with all its possible downfalls, was perfect. We stayed in the library and worked until lunchtime, then we migrated as a group to the coffee shop. It was time for Preston to start his shift, so he pushed a bunch of tables together for us.

After lunch, we all went our separate ways. I had to work. Oliver went with me. Gretchen had deliveries to make and asked Oliver if he could watch the cash register for her while she was gone. It was usually a task I did myself between filling my own orders, but Gretchen knew I hated it. Oliver's kind, people friendly personality was much better suited for the job.

I stood at the counter, swaying my hips to the music from the radio in Gretchen's office. Oliver peeked his head around the corner. "What are you making tonight?"

I grinned over my shoulder at him. "Something new."

He immediately rounded the corner. "New?"

Oliver tried to sneak a look into the bowl, but I pulled it away. "No looking."

I found a clean spoon in the drawer and dipped a small sample of my new icing onto the end. "Open up. Tell what you think it is simply by the taste."

Oliver closed his eyes and opened his mouth. "I love this game."

He took the bite then sank against the counter. "Oh my gosh, that's good. That tastes like these orange Creamsicle ice creams pops I used to eat as a kid."

"That is exactly what I was shooting for. I'm going to make a vanilla orange swirl cake with this on the top."

"Tonight?"

I laughed. "Yes. Tonight."

"Are you going to make extra? In case you mess up, or your boyfriend steals them, right?"

"Yes. There will be a couple extra."

Oliver took a seat on the stool next to the counter and made himself comfortable, and I continued to work. The cupcakes in the freezer should be cooled down by now, which meant a few final whips on my new icing, and everything would be ready for the final steps. Oliver picked up a spatula and spun it around. "Have you heard from your dad anymore?"

My head popped up. My immediate response told me to lie. I didn't want to lie to my boyfriend, though. I also didn't want him to know my father continued to call and now text me every day with very strict instructions to send him my grades.

The texts and voicemails weren't as nice as they

used to be. The one he sent yesterday stated something along the lines of it being my last warning. Finals were next week, though, and I could just show him my final grades for the class. I could endure the lecture of five A's and one B. There still might be a chance I could beg his forgiveness and manage to stay at Maryland next year.

There would be no hope if he saw that midterm grade, though. No hope at all.

I just had to avoid him for one more week. "He's been in touch," I said stiffly. "I'll be glad to have this semester over and behind me."

Oliver fiddled with the other utensils on the counter to keep from looking at me. "How is your relationship with him? You don't really talk about him…well…at all."

I stared down in the bowl in front of me. "My father is different." I paused, trying to find words that didn't make him sound horrifying, which would be the truth. "Very difficult most of the time."

"Like how?"

I set the bowl down and went to retrieve my cupcakes from the freezer. I'd never discussed my father with anyone before. Not even Sloan or Ava. They knew my mother had left us, but I couldn't bear to admit the one parent I did have acted as if I was a complete and total failure all the time, even though Sloan figured it out for herself.

Oliver got up from his seat. "Are you afraid of him?"

I glanced up. "No."

My voiced sounded off. It sounded like a total

lie. "He's not abusive to me," I added.

Oliver's fingers grazed my elbow. "There are other types of abuse than just physical abuse, Elle. I see that look in your eyes every time your phone rings. Just now, when I mentioned him, your entire body froze up."

"He's just strict with me."

Oliver held me in place. "How?"

"The normal things. If everyone else's curfew was eleven o'clock, then mine was nine. Everyone else got to drive to school, and he dropped me off at the front door."

Oliver held my gaze. "And what are the not normal things?"

I bit my lip.

He knew.

Oliver knew what was wrong without me having to tell him. Was it really that obvious? Did Sloan and Ava notice it too? Was my shame that easy to see?

I looked away.

"Eloise..."

"My clothes were always a big deal," I said, my voice already breaking. "Everything was always too revealing, or too tight. I could wear jeans and a t-shirt and he'd accuse me of going out to try to hook up with guys. And dating...well, dating was impossible. No boy was ever good enough. He either didn't like their parents, or heard these ridiculous rumors. He always had a reason for why I couldn't go."

It hurt saying it out loud. Because I knew, even as I tried to explain it away to myself, how he treated me was wrong.

"He wouldn't let me eat sweets. For Christmas last year, he gave me a gym membership, and said it was for my own good. He gave me a debit card. I was never allowed to use cash. That way he knew exactly what I spent my money on and he could analyze it at length."

Oliver touched my cheek, and my words started coming out as sobs. "He told me the reason I needed to graduate top of my class was because girls who looked like me had to work twice as hard."

Oliver kissed me.

His hand knotted in my hair, and his lips, urgent and all consuming, found mine.

"He's wrong." Oliver gasped the words between kisses. "You know he's wrong, right?"

I did now.

I pressed my face into Oliver's shoulder and held him. What I didn't tell Oliver was what my father would surely think of him. I'd never been allowed to date. *You'd just end up like your mother.* I didn't know how long I stayed there like that. Time didn't seem to matter. At some point, Gretchen returned from her deliveries, and I finally let Oliver go to finish my cupcakes. He stayed close to me, though. Only inches separated us.

We didn't talk any more about it. I thought Oliver could tell I'd reached my emotional capacity for one day. What I told him was only the tip of the iceberg of Bartholomew Duncan. After I finished my shift, he walked back to my apartment with me. Oliver found a recipe for chicken lasagna, and he wanted to try it. As in, Oliver wanted to cook me dinner. He said he'd been studying the recipe and he thought, with my expert guidance, he could manage it.

I looked forward to watching him try. Either way—good, bad, or burnt to a crisp—I would eat it. We stopped at the grocery store and picked up everything we needed then went to my apartment. Sometime in between my putting my stuff up and grabbing a ponytail holder for my hair, Oliver had found my Betty Boop apron and made himself at home in my kitchen. I made myself comfortable on the couch and started up our *Superman* marathon we didn't get to finish the other night. I bypassed the West years and went straight to present day Henry Cavill.

"Hey, Elle, can I use this to stir up stuff?" Oliver stood at the edge of the kitchen counter holding an apple peeler.

I pointed toward the utensil holder next to the fridge. "You'd have better luck with the whisk."

He looked over his shoulder. "And a whisk looks like…"

I rolled my eyes and pushed play on the movie before going to join him. Someone had to teach the poor boy to cook. It might as well be me. I slapped his butt. "Move over, Boop. Let me teach you how to work your way around a kitchen."

Oliver and I cooked dinner together. He did all the manual labor, and I guided him. We ate lasagna on the floor in front of the television like two kids watching Saturday morning cartoons.

The doorbell rang the same time Oliver placed

our dishes in the sink. He started to turn on the water, but paused. I remained seated in my spot on the floor, plotting how to get him to take his shirt off. The doorbell rang again. "Are you going to answer that?"

I shrugged. "It's probably Sloan." And she could wait. She could turn into one of those little stone gnomes, for all I cared. Oliver laughed as a loud knock echoed through my apartment. "That sounds urgent. What if she needs you?"

I eyed him. "You're too nice. We're going to have to work on that."

I dragged myself off the couch and to the door. I swung it open, prepared to scowl at my friend before giving her a lecture. Except it wasn't Sloan.

My mouth dropped open. "Dad?"

It was definitely him. Six feet, three inches of power suit and anger. My father pressed his lips tightly together, his features stern and unyielding. "Well, look who is alive. It's my daughter who I had to fly across the country to see and make sure she wasn't dead in a ditch somewhere."

I winced. Crap. I really should have sent that message to his secretary. "Dad, I'm sorry. I can explain."

He stepped past me, but I grabbed his arm. His dark eyes looked down at me, glaring at the point where my hand touched his arm. "You're lucky I don't put you on a plane back home this instant."

"I told you I can explain."

"I've called you, Eloise...for weeks. No answer. I've left you voicemails. I even called the university. They said they couldn't tell me whether you've shown up to class or not. I had to cancel three meetings to fly out here and check on you."

I tried to hold him back, but it was too late. He was in the door. Oliver stood in the middle of the living room. My dad paused as soon as he saw him. This was bad. So terribly bad.

He glanced at me then back at Oliver. "Who are you?"

Oliver swallowed. I instinctively jumped in front of him. "This is Oliver. He's my tutor."

"Your tutor?"

I moved further in front of Oliver in hope my dad wouldn't notice the dishes, the movie playing, and the total lack of books anywhere in sight. "Yeah. He's been helping me study. We were just about to start."

"You were going to study?" His voice dropped. "Well, then, let me see your midterm grades. I want to know how well this tutoring has been working."

"We only started this week." I was horrible at lying, especially to my dad.

"Your grades, Eloise. I want to see them. You think I wouldn't notice how you suddenly stop answering my calls the same week your grades were to be issued?"

Of course he noticed. He'd probably been waiting for the opportunity for weeks. "Midterms don't matter."

He set his features straight. "They matter to me."

I took a deep breath, tears already welling in my eyes. Worst nightmare didn't even begin to explain the gut wrenching knots that twisted in my stomach. I walked over and found the college issued stock paper I'd stuck in a drawer by my desk. I handed it to him. He read down the paper. "You're failing."

"It's one class, and I've already brought the grade up."

"This is unacceptable." He threw the paper down on my desk. "You're transferring at the end of the semester."

"I can bring it up." My gaze dropped to the floor.

"To what, Eloise? To a C? Those kinds of grades won't get you into—"

"I'm not going to graduate school." I tried to make my voice sound strong. I tried to be confident. "I know that's your plan for me. To eventually make me change my major and follow your route to success, but it isn't *my* plan."

I sounded more like a ten-year-old who'd been caught with their hand in the cookie jar.

My father flexed his fingers across the back of my computer chair. "Tell your friend to leave, Eloise."

I bit my lip. I couldn't take it anymore. I couldn't take him telling me what to do. Eighteen years, he'd controlled me. Every aspect of my life. I couldn't take it anymore. This tiny piece of freedom I'd gained since coming to college only proved how much more of it I needed. "No."

Oliver took a step forward. "Elle, maybe your dad is right. I should go. For now."

I gritted my teeth. I didn't want to agree to anything my father suggested. "I said no."

My father's eyes lit up with fire, but I held my stance. I lifted my chin and looked Bartholomew directly in the eye. "You can leave."

His chin set tight. "You think I won't put you on a plane this afternoon? You—"

"I'm legally an adult. You can't make me do anything anymore."

"I pay your tuition."

"Not anymore. I'll quit school before I take another dime from you."

My father laughed.

Laughed.

As if standing up for myself was some kind of joke. "Do you think you're impressing him right now?"

"Leave Oliver out of this."

"You've always been so much like her."

Her. He wouldn't even say my mother's name. I guessed "her" was better than the explicative he usually used to describe the woman he was supposed to love.

"Leave my mother out of it too. This isn't about anyone but me and you."

He rolled his eyes. "You're going to end up just like her. Some two-bit airhead, sulking around bars hoping to get knocked up by the first decent man with a job."

He always did this too—degraded her. He'd been introduced to my mother at a bar by a mutual friend. To hear him tell it, she'd come there for the sole purpose of getting pregnant with me so she could trap him into marrying her.

Because—you know—he was such a catch and all.

"I'm tired. Do you realize that? I'm tired of this same argument. That's why I didn't send you my grades, because I didn't want to have this same fight. The same one we have every single time I don't follow your rules." I threw my hands in the air, my voice breaking. "And you know what…maybe I am like her. Maybe I want to be like her. She was strong enough to leave you. Maybe all I want is that same strength. Just to be enough like her to escape you."

"You ungrateful—" He spun around, marching across the room. "I should have let her take you."

"Take me?"

"Go on—fail your classes. End up on the street."

I stepped closer to him. "What do you mean by you should have let her take me?"

He pointed at me, words on the tip of his tongue, but he didn't say them.

My voice broke. "Answer me. Did she try to take me with her?"

His eyes narrowed as he turned toward the door.

"Look at me." My voice was a shrill scream now.

His expression, his stance. Everything about my father in that instant should have induced fear. He wouldn't cross that line, though, not in front of Oliver. That was the secret to his success. He only allowed me to see the *real* him. The world saw the hardworking, single father who doted on his honor roll daughter every chance he got. He reserved the rest of him, the dark part that rooted itself deep inside of him, just for me.

He pulled a piece of paper out of his pocket and slammed it on the table next to me. It was a plane ticket. He'd already bought it. He never planned to let me stay. "It leaves tonight. You be on it."

I was very lucky Oliver stayed. The glare in his eye pretty much screamed it at me. He would have made me go. Physically made me. He stormed out without another word.

Oliver's hand touched my shoulder, but I could barely feel it. "Elle?"

"She wanted to take me with her."

His hand gripped my shoulder, and I fell to the floor.

"She wanted to take me with her."

He pulled me against his chest. "It's okay. It's going to be okay."

Tears brimmed over my lashes. "I could have been with her this whole time."

Every dream...every fantasy I ever had of being with my mom hurt so much worse now. It could have been real. We could have had that loft apartment in the city. We could have spent our mornings baking. I could have had someone to share my secrets with, and shop for my prom dress. I could have had someone to celebrate my accomplishments instead of expect them with the fear of the consequence looming over my head.

I could have been free.

Happy.

I clenched my hand in the front of Oliver's shirt and pushed away. I didn't want him to meet my father. I didn't want him to know some part of that man somehow existed inside of me.

"No." Oliver tried to pull me back. "Stay with me. We can talk about this."

We couldn't. How could I in good conscience

subject Oliver to that man?

"I can't. I can't do this."

"Yes, Elle. You can. I'm here. Talk to me."

"I think I just need to be alone right now."

"No. That's what he wants. He wants this to push you away from me."

I got up, and Oliver grabbed my hand. "He wants to isolate you, Eloise. He wants to keep you away from anyone who might actually love you. He saw it on my face as soon as he walked in the door. I was a threat. He knew it."

It was too much.

My breath lodged in my throat.

My hands kept slipping out of his, and then I realized it was because I kept pulling away. My feet moved backward, toward the door.

"Stay with me, Eloise." Oliver's face. His perfect, beautiful face. "We can fix this, sweetie. Stay."

Wrong.

Everything about it felt wrong. Panic ate at me. It devoured me.

What would I do now?

Suddenly, Oliver's hands were on my shoulders. Pressing down. "Calm down, baby. Slow your breathing. You're going to hyperventilate."

His words…that look on his face…it choked me.

"I need to be alone."

Alone. Just how my father wanted it.

Chapter
Twenty-Three

GLORIOUS REALITY

The black tulle that stuck out underneath the hem of my halter dress scratched against my bare knees. I sat on the floor of the kitchen at Sugar Cube, my recipe book gripped in my arms. I knew my father too well. If I went back to California with him, he'd find a way to wipe away my bake shop dream. He probably already had me an internship set up with his company and applications waiting for my graduate degree.

Yes. I considered it. It was engrained in my head. You didn't defy my father. You might try to defy him, but in the end, you did what he said.

Tears wet my eyelashes as I tried not to think about my future. I didn't want to leave this place. Sugar Cube and Gretchen had become my fantasy family. I didn't want to lose her, or her words of wisdom and constant inspiration. I needed someone like Gretchen in my life to keep the crazy teenage side of me in check while still giving me enough room to grow and learn from my own mistakes.

Then there were my friends. What would I do without a Sloan and an Ava in California? I wasn't exactly the easiest person to get to know, and if you managed to bypass the exterior turn offs, there was my quirky sense of humor and off the wall antics to deal with. Friends like them didn't pop out of thin air.

I couldn't bring myself to think about Oliver. There wasn't another Oliver Edwards in the entire world. He was irreplaceable. A nerd who loved my cupcakes as much as I loved making them. I wasn't naïve enough to think something couldn't go wrong with our barely new relationship, but I've never wanted to take the chance on heartbreak as much as I did with him. The risk finally outweighed the cost.

It was very simple. There was no going back. Bartholomew Duncan couldn't be in my life anymore. Oliver was right. My father isolated me. He hid me away from anyone who might actually offer me the love and attention I needed to function. The love that would inspire my defeated willpower to defy him.

He'd kept me away from my mother. That alone was unforgiveable.

There was a soft knock on the door behind me. I didn't look up. I saw the toes of Oliver's Chuck Taylors standing in the doorframe. I couldn't even bear to look at him. I didn't want to see everything I was about to lose.

"May I come in?"

I sobbed.

Even after witnessing everything at my apartment. Even after I left him standing there alone. Oliver was here.

I glanced up, my vision blurred, but I could still see him. His hair was slightly more chaotic than it had been at my apartment earlier. A green jacket covered his black shirt with a giant replica of the periodic table on it. In his arms he held a couple notebooks and what looked like my anatomy book. His hand touched the place on his chest where his heart would be.

I stared down at my recipe book. "I'm sorry."

Oliver's gaze dropped to me as he bent down in front of me. "You don't have to apologize to me, Elle."

"I do, actually. I shouldn't have left."

He touched my cheek. "You were overwhelmed. It's understandable."

Forgiveness. Acceptance. I wasn't accustomed to these things.

I wiped away a stray tear. "My mother left when I was only a kid. I thought she was so desperate to get away from him that she didn't think about me. I didn't know she'd tried to take me with her." I bit my lip at the harsh truth of it. "I was nothing more than a bargaining chip to him. He thought if he kept me, she would come back."

Oliver took his hand in mine, setting his books down beside me.

I squeezed it, intertwining my fingers with his. "I'm glad she didn't come back. You know, for her sake."

"Is he why you were so worried about your grade? Because you were literally afraid to tell him?"

I nodded. "You heard him. He's been looking for an excuse to make me come back home. I knew he would use my grade against me. I'm over it, though. I meant what I said. I'll either find a way to pay my tuition myself, or I'll quit."

Oliver moved over beside me and sat against the wall. His ankle connected with mine as he playfully knocked his heel against the toe of my bare foot. I'd discarded my shoes in the corner when I came in.

"I hope you don't mind, but I took a peek at your grades when you left. You made a 4.0 last semester, and you're doing amazing in all your other classes. If we brought your grade up, you'd be eligible to apply for a scholarship for next year."

"I can't possibly bring my grade up to an A, Oliver. It's statistically impossible."

"Actually," he said, scooting his glasses up his nose, "it's not impossible. Improbable, because it would mean you making a perfect grade on the final, but it can be done."

I peered over at the stack of books he'd brought with him. "You think I could do that?"

Oliver held my hand between both his, bringing it up to his lips. He placed a soft kiss across my knuckles. "I think you can do anything you want to do, Elle."

I got up and set my recipe book on the table. "I have other classes. I have projects due, and the final exams in English and calculus won't be a walk in the park. Then I have work, and..."

"You can do it." Oliver pulled himself to his feet, placed his hands on my hips, and pulled me toward him. "I know you can, and I'll help you."

"We will all help you."

I peeked over Oliver's shoulder to find Sloan, Ava, Preston, Brad, and Gretchen all huddled just outside the door. I shot an accusing look at him. "You called them?"

"Of course, I called them." He smiled like it should have been obvious. "We're not willing to let you fail. We'll get you a scholarship for next year."

"That's right," Sloan said, coming over to me. "And we'll move in together next year. It'll save us both money that we can put toward books."

Gretchen walked over to my side. "And you know you always have a job here."

I looked around at all their faces. They believed in me. They cared about me unconditionally. "I can do this," I said confidently.

Oliver hugged me. "I know you can."

For the first in my life, I believed it. I believed in myself.

***

The ten o'clock flight out of DC to Los Angeles left with one empty seat.

Chapter Twenty-Four

ESCAPE

I walked into Rowdy Randy's with my head held high. I carried a simple white envelope, and inside it were my final grades. I hadn't looked at them yet. Oliver sat waiting for me on a stool at the bar. I came up behind him and ran my hand across his shoulder. "Well, don't you look fetching?"

He glanced back at me and smiled. His tux was pristine. Solid black with a perfect bowtie. He'd tamed his hair as much as he could manage it. In his case, that probably took a lot of effort. "Thank you."

He straightened his tie. "You look pretty spectacular yourself."

I twirled around in my new red sequined dress. It fit like a glove over my generous curves. I had an event later this afternoon. Gretchen had signed me up to be a vendor at the largest wedding event in the state. I had a cupcake wedding cake I would display for all the soon-to-be brides and wedding planners to see. Thousands would be in attendance, which meant major publicity for Cupcakes by Eloise.

I curtsied. "Thank you, kind sir."

He pointed at the envelope. "Have you checked it yet?"

I placed the envelope on the counter. "Don't worry about the grades. They'll be there tomorrow."

He raised a brow, and I leaned into him.

"So, I don't know if anyone has told you, but I'm kind of a big deal."

He leaned back and laughed. "Oh, really?"

"Yep. If you play your cards right, I might even give you my autograph."

"Your autograph, huh?"

"Yep. It's really unique. It's ten digits."

Oliver's grin covered his entire face. "So, what does a guy need to do for that kind A-list treatment?"

The bartender came by and set my favorite drink, a tequila sunrise in front of me. Oliver must have ordered it for me before I arrived. I held it up. "This is a good start. This will at least get you the area code."

Oliver reached over and grabbed the envelope. "The suspense is killing me. Do you mind if I peek?"

I shrugged and downed a gulp of the drink. "Sure. I don't care what it says. If I don't get that scholarship, I will just take out loans like every other student in America." My father's way wasn't the only way. I would choose my own path from now on.

He hadn't called or contacted me in any way since he stormed out of my apartment that night. He'd cut off my debit card, though, so I had to open my own account and set up to have all my paychecks auto delivered to it.

I would not fall to his tactics. He wouldn't starve me out. There was nothing he could take away from me that I wouldn't give up to keep my new life just the way it was.

Oliver slid his finger under the envelope's edge and tore it open. I twirled my straw around in the frozen ice as he unfolded it. Funny how I no longer felt that foreboding sense of dread. So, what if I only managed to bring it up to a C? The world would go on. I'd learn from it, and do better next semester. In the end, I would get the same degree as the people who graduated top of the class.

Oliver read down the paper then very carefully folded it up.

"Well," I said, nodding toward the paper that he placed back into the envelope. "What did it say?"

He smirked. "I thought you didn't care."

"I care. It's just different now. I care for myself."

He handed the envelope over to me. "You should see it for yourself."

I took the paper, ripped it out of the envelope, and opened it. I scanned the sheet, checking to make sure my for-sure classes were, in fact, the grade I expected them to be before moving down to the one that counted.

Introduction to Anatomy: B

I smiled.

Yes. Smiled.

I had never in my life been so proud of a B.

"Oh my god. I can't believe I actually did it."

Oliver touched my elbow. "So, you're not disappointed?"

I shook the paper at him. "Are you kidding me? I had a 58 at midterms. This is a miraculous accomplishment."

Oliver grinned. "It is. I'm very proud of you."

"This probably means I won't get the scholarship, but you know what...life goes on. It will be okay. The world isn't going end."

"You know what?" Oliver stood and hugged me. "I totally agree. In fact, your optimism has inspired me."

"Really? To do what?"

His gaze ran down my skintight dress. "How much time did you say we had until the event started?"

I elbowed him playfully. "Only an hour now."

His face fell and I hugged him tighter. "Afterward, though...I'm all yours."

Oliver and I enjoyed our drinks together, raising a toast to my hard earned B. We arrived at the event early. It was held upstairs in the convention center. Over three hundred vendors were set up, ranging from bakeries, florists, DJs, and everything else a bride might even consider for her wedding. I was determined to make us stand out. Cupcakes by Eloise went for high glamour. Oliver and Sloan were my waiters who would carry around platters of bitesize cupcakes for everyone to sample. I stood next to my giant wedding cake display, prepared to answer questions. Gretchen and Ava handed out flyers and information packets about all our stuff available at the bakery.

My hands turned clammy as people started arriving. Ava snuck over toward me and handed me a glass of sparkling wine. "Here. I stole it from one of other vendors. I thought you could use something to calm your nerves."

I took the drink and pulled her into my side. "You never know. There are a lot of cake vendors here. I may not have to talk to anyone tonight."

Ava knocked her hip into mine. "I really hope you're wrong."

They opened the doors, and people started filing into the banquet room. We had a prime spot in the corner at the end of the first row. Gretchen clapped her hands to get our attention. "Everyone to your spots. It's game time."

Ava gave me another quick hug, but she disappeared behind the table with her information packets.

I was dead wrong about not getting any visitors to our table. I must have talked to every bride at the event. My cupcake wedding cake was a hit. Ava scrambled behind the curtain to put more packets together because everyone who stopped by wanted pricing information, and several dozen went ahead and set up appointments to come in and book their cake.

Two hours into the event, I was mentally

exhausted. Gretchen took my spot to let me slip off and take a break. I moved over to the next table, which happened to be a catering service. They were giving away free samples of pasta. I grabbed a plate and found a quiet spot in the corner. Maybe some food in my stomach would help.

It wasn't as stressful as predicted. As it turned out, I still didn't like to talk to strangers, but if I must talk to them, talking about baking was the most acceptable way.

"Excuse me?"

I looked over my shoulder, and a woman stood at the edge of the table holding one of my flyers. "The lady down there said you were Eloise."

I nodded.

The woman had honey blonde hair. It was thin and dangled down her shoulder. She smiled softly. "I tested your cupcakes, and I have to say, I immediately fell in love."

Now I smiled. Anyone who said the words love and cupcakes in the same sentence immediately became okay in my book on the spot. "Thank you. Are you getting married soon?"

She smiled. "Yes. The end of the summer, actually."

"Well, we're having a summer sale if you're interested in any of our services at Sugar Cube."

"The wedding is in Italy."

My shoulders slumped a little. "Oh. Well, unfortunately I don't think I can ship cupcakes there."

"Yes, well, I kind of figured that. My wedding isn't exactly why I came to talk to you."

"Oh." I set my plate down and wiped my hands on my napkin. "Is there something else I could help you with?"

"You're Eloise."

I looked strangely at her. "Yes."

"Eloise Duncan?"

"Yes," I said a little more cautiously this time.

The lady laughed. "I mean, of course you are. Look at that hair. It's just like I remember it."

Her eyes. They weren't quite green or brown. *Hazel*. I knew those eyes.

My fingers touched my mouth, holding in the gasp. "Mom?"

Tears welled up in her eyes. "Ellie, darling."

I clutched my heart. She had paint stained fingertips and a long kaleidoscope dress. Was that a streak of blue in her hair? "Oh my god. It's really you."

Now she covered her mouth, her fingers trembling. "You're so beautiful."

I grabbed the table for support. Oliver noticed. He set down his platter of cupcakes and watched us. I spoke very quietly. "What are you doing here?"

"Your father called me."

"What? Why?"

"He said he was done. He said there was no saving you from turning into me. He sent me your address."

I could have been angry. There was something to be said about her putting up more of a fight against him so she could have taken me with her. The anger wasn't inside me, though. I couldn't muster an ounce of it. The only thing inside me was pure, unadulterated joy. I ran to her. "Thank you."

I hugged her. I took in the scent of her soft perfume, the crafted metal earrings she wore, and the jeweled pin in her hair. This was really her. *My* mother.

Oliver stepped into view. His worried expression made me laugh. I turned to him, laughing hysterically. "This is my mother."

His eyes rounded. I hugged her again. "This is Celeste..." Then I paused, because I didn't know whether or not she'd kept Duncan as her last name or switched it back to her maiden name.

"Montgomery," she answered for me.

Ah. Yes, so she'd switched. I liked it better.

I tried again. "This is my mother, Celeste Montgomery."

Oliver came over and shook her hand as he continued to steal glances at me. He looked as if he was afraid I might shatter into a millions pieces at any moment. And I just might.

"It's nice to meet you."

I looked at my mother and smiled back at Oliver. "And this is my boyfriend, Oliver Edwards."

"It's nice to meet you too, Oliver."

The others started to gather around as well. So I introduced them. I introduced my mother to every single person I cared about in the world, and it felt awesome. After a round of hellos, my mother grabbed my hand. "Oh, Ellie. I had no idea how this would go, but I knew I had to find you." She touched my hair, my face. Her voice broke. "I've missed you. I've missed everything about you."

I laughed as the tears spilled over my lashes.

"Ditto."

She laughed with me. Nothing about it was funny. It was merely the happiness radiating out of us in the only way it knew how. "Please, sweetheart, don't cry. I don't want to ruin your night."

"You could never ruin it. You've made this night even better than I thought it could be."

She held up the flyer in her hand. "I do want you to make the cake for my wedding. I know it's soon, and I know I have a lot of forgiveness to earn, but I want you with me, Ellie. I want my daughter with me."

"You want to fly me to Italy?"

"Yes. You can bring your boyfriend and your friends. You can bring whoever. I want to spend time with you. I don't want to miss another moment of your life, and I want you in every part of mine. Say you'll give me a chance. Tell me you'll let me make up for everything that man stole from us."

I nodded. I couldn't stop nodding. "Of course."

And I meant it. I had everything I ever wanted. I would never let it go.

Chapter Twenty-Five

CONFESSIONS

Oliver Edwards stood in the doorway of my temporary bedroom at the Italian cottage. My mother had insisted on buying us all tickets to come to her wedding. The room was quaint and homey. We'd been there for three days, enjoying the beautiful confines of the vineyard and surrounding areas. The sun beamed through the open window into the room as it started to set over the horizon. He'd rolled the sleeves of his pinstriped shirt up to his elbows. He'd trimmed his hair before our overseas adventure, so it now stood perfectly on end. He stuck one hand in his pocket and adjusted his glasses with the other. I strutted over to him, eyeing him coyly.

"Suspenders? Really?"

He pulled them out to showcase them. "What?

All the other groomsmen are wearing them."

I tugged my silky white robe tighter around me. "Well, this bridesmaid might not make it to the wedding if you don't hide your sexy self somewhere."

"You're already running late," he said, leaning against the doorframe. "I've been sent to fetch you."

I walked back over to the mirror and placed the last pin in my hair. "All I have to do is put my dress on."

Oliver's smile grew. "I showed up just in time."

I smiled over my shoulder at him. "In fact, you did. I could use some help."

"Where are Sloan and Ava? I thought they were supposed to be helping you."

"I sent them on. I was kind of hoping you'd stop by."

Oliver stood, his eyes studying me. "If you're commando under that robe, we're going to miss the wedding."

I got my dress down off the hanger. "Tempting, but that's not what I wanted to talk to you about."

Oliver came and stood behind me and looked at the mirror. "What is it?"

I squeezed his hand that he laid on my shoulder. "I'm glad you're here."

He cocked his head. "Where else would I be?"

I turned to face him. "This summer has been insane. Between helping me move into Sloan's apartment, fulfilling all those new cupcake orders during wedding season, countless dinners and outings with my mom and her fiancé, to flying around the world to this wedding, you've gone above and beyond your boyfriend duties."

"No, see, that's where you're wrong." He placed his lips right at the edge of my ear. "Everything I've done, everything I will do, is because you deserve it."

A light tap on the door caught my attention, and I looked over Oliver's shoulder. It was my mother. Her hair was down, hanging in waves across her shoulders. She wore a beautiful, cream dress that fell to the floor. "Oh. Wow."

She smiled at the sight of us. "Am I interrupting?"

I kept Oliver's hand in mine and looked back at him. I couldn't take my eyes off him. I was in love.

Real love.

It started as this silly crush, but now, I loved him. Oliver pulled me into his side and kissed my cheek. "I was trying to hurry her up."

My mother laughed as she came to us. "She comes by it naturally."

I hadn't noticed it, but she carried a small white box in her hand. She held it up to me. "I have something for you. I would love it if you wore it today for the ceremony, and then it's yours to keep."

"A present? For me?"

She opened the lid of the box and held it over for me to see. It was a slender silver chain, and attached to the end was a tiny locket. A cursive "M" could be seen engraved in the center. "Every woman in the Montgomery family has worn it for ages. I had it saved for you for your sixteenth birthday, but today seems just as fitting."

251

I pulled out the necklace, my heart beaming with pride. "I love it. Thank you."

Oliver held his hand out. "Would you like for me to help you put it on?"

"Yes, please."

Oliver latched the necklace, and I held the locket between my fingers, admiring its beauty. Someone cleared their throat at the door, and I turned around. It was Brett, my mother's fiancé. We'd grown quite close over the summer. He was absolutely perfect for her, in the all the same ways Oliver was perfect for me. He smiled.

"The minister is waiting," he said with a laugh.

My mother gave me a quick kiss. "Get dressed and I'll meet you out on the deck in ten minutes."

I nodded, my voice too strained to risk speaking again. Too full of emotion. My mother joined Brett, giving me one more smile over her shoulder. Oliver unzipped my garment bag and removed the sheer pink lace dress from the hanger. I sniffed at the sight of it.

"You're not going to make it through the ceremony without crying on me, are you?"

I shook my head.

I took off my robe and took my dress. Oliver helped me zip up the back. I twirled around, enjoying how the end flared at the motion. Oliver's eyes danced at the sight of me. "You look amazing, but then again, you always do."

Everything about this moment felt like a dream. This place. Us. "I love you."

I said it. I'd meant it for a while now, but I honestly didn't know if I had it in me to say it. I'd never said it to a boy before, and Oliver was the only boy I ever wanted to say it to.

He held his breath. His fingertips touched my hair then my lips. "I love you too, Eloise."

He kissed me.

Oliver Edwards kissed me. He loved me too.

"Excuse us."

I pulled away from Oliver's lips just enough to glare at the door. Sloan and Ava stood inside the frame, grinning. "What did I tell you two about interrupting us?"

Ava rolled her eyes. "This isn't the poetry section."

Sloan smiled as she stepped inside. "The bride and groom are waiting."

I straightened Oliver's shirt and adjusted his tie. "Afterward," I said again, remembering my promise from earlier in the day when we sneaked through the vineyard together.

"Afterward," he agreed. He bent down to whisper in my ear. "Though I would like a dance with you at the reception first."

I leaned back and eyed him. "You dance?"

"You don't know everything about me yet. I still have a few surprises up my sleeve."

I tugged at his suspenders. "Indeed."

Ava cleared her throat. "We're waiting," she sang.

I glared at them again. "Fine." I looked back at Oliver. "Let's go before we miss it."

We walked hand in hand out to the deck where we met my mother and Brett. My soon to be stepfather had brought his son and daughter to take part in the ceremony as well. Preston stood with Sloan and Ava. Brad did not make the trip. Ava's baseball player love affair had fizzled out soon after the semester ended. She seemed to be recovering quite well, though. She eyed my future stepbrother, who I'd been told played baseball at Michigan, with interest.

Yes, Ava Morrison would be just fine without Brad.

We walked through the vineyard as a group to a secluded spot in the garden that looked out over the rolling hills of the countryside. It was there, as the sun set low in the sky, creating a soft orange glow over the lush green of the vineyard, that my mother and Brett said their vows.

Oliver held my hand through it all. And I couldn't help but smile.

It was true confession time.

I, Eloise Duncan, finally understood happiness, contentment, and love.

I felt it. I lived it. I soaked it into every fiber of my being. Standing there on the hill, with my family, friends, and of course, my Oliver, at my side, I wasn't naïve enough to believe life wouldn't still throw me a wrench every now and then. But with these people, and their support, I would make it through it all.

No more fear.

No more hiding away in the shadows watching the world go by.

I was ready to face it. Instead of imagining dreams…I wanted to make them come true.

And I would. One nerdy kiss and cupcake at a

time.

Acknowledgements

Thank you to my family for working so hard to make writing a possibility for me. I have the absolute best support system in the world. A special thank you to my husband John and my friends Whitney and Kim. Thanks for always understanding my quirky sense of humor and for being the only people not surprised by the silliness that I write. Thank you to my daughters, Delilah and Gracie for sharing in the excitement of each book birthday with me as if it were your own birthday.

A special thank you to the entire Limitless Publishing team. You are all rock stars and I couldn't be happier to have you guys on my side. You make a complicated process seem so effortless.

And a big thank you to every single person who reads this book. Sharing a part of yourself with the world is hard, but those of you who take time out your day to encourage a writer make this grueling process worth it.

About the Author

Savannah was born in Hyden, Kentucky. She received her M.S in Speech Language Pathology from The University of Mississippi in 2009. She's been writing since the early age of nine when she begged her parents for a type writer for Christmas.

She now lives in Corbin, Ky with her husband of eight years, John, and their two wonderful daughters, Delilah and Gracie.

When she isn't working, or running after her kids, she spends her free time traveling the country with her husband. There is nothing better than a day of football in the grove, a late night of basketball at Rupp Arena or slapping the glass to celebrate another Washington Capitals goal.

She is a strong believer that with enough hard work and determination you can accomplish anything.

Facebook:
https://www.facebook.com/savannahblevinsauthor

Twitter:
https://twitter.com/vannajodee

Website:
http://www.savannahblevins.com/

Made in the USA
San Bernardino, CA
01 February 2017